IT HAD TO BE VIGILANTES

The hangings were clearly of a particularly cruel form. The rope would be secured to the big branch about twenty feet above the ground and the vigilantes would ride off, simply leaving their victim to stare his own death in the face and wait...

How long depended on the temperament of the horse. Minutes would pass slowly. The broiling sun beat down as the victim sat tensely waiting any movement of the horse beneath him. Night would come and then day.

Finally hunger and thirst would force the horse to abandon the weight on its back. The animal would start to walk, the man would slide off the saddle into space, slowly strangling at the end of the rope.

OTHER BOOKS BY JAKE LOGAN

JAKE LOGAN

SLOCUM AND THE HANGING TREE

BERKLEY BOOKS, NEW YORK

SLOCUM AND THE HANGING TREE

A Berkley Book/published by arrangement with
the author

PRINTING HISTORY
Berkley edition/July 1988

ISBN: 0-425-10935-6

A BERKLEY BOOK ® TM 757,375
Berkley Books are published by The Berkley Publishing Group
200 Madison Avenue, New York, N.Y. 10016.
The name "BERKLEY" and the "B" logo
are trademarks belonging to Berkley Publishing Corporation.

PRINTED IN THE UNITED STATES OF AMERICA

10 9 8 7 6 5 4 3 2 1

1

They were five, those riders. They were terrible men. Anybody could have seen that as they drew rein and sat their horses outside the town.

Silently they regarded the cluster of low wooden buildings as the eastern sky darkened, while behind them a brilliant sunset stained the sky. Their faces, dark beneath their dusty, trail beaten Stetson hats, were hard, expressionless. They sat their horses stiffly, leaning just a little forward, alert for instant action. Their mounts, too, were motionless, sensing the tension in the men.

From someplace in the town came the sound of a creaking door, the rattle of a bucket. Nobody was in sight, yet lights had started in a couple of the buildings. Now one of the riders cursed aimlessly and spat over his horse's head. Another started to reach to his shirt pocket for his makings but then changed his mind and let his hand drop to the worn butt of the holstered sixgun at his side.

Leather creaked, a bit jangled as the group of five began to walk their horses toward the main street of the town. There was still no one at that end of the street; only a spotted dog with a chewed-up ear who suddenly appeared from an alley, took one look at the grim caval- cade of men and guns, and skedaddled.

At this time most of the citizens were at supper; the visitors had counted on this. They dismounted outside the Pastime, wrapping their reins around the hitch rail with a horse knot so that a quick pull would free the animal instantly.

They stayed close together as they stepped onto the boardwalk and walked to the front of Carrigan's General Store. One man was wearing spurs and as his heavy boots hit the boardwalk they jangled into the silent town. Somewhere a door slammed and the sound of a man's laughter rushed into the street.

They had planned it, and no talking was necessary. Three remained outside the store on the boardwalk, with their backs to the building. Coldly they eyed the lighted windows on the other side of the street.

The other two entered the store, pausing just inside the door to let their eyes get used to the lamplight. There were four people inside. A clerk was waiting on two customers, while Clyde Carrigan was at the rear of the store counting the day's money. One of the cus- tomers, a fat man named Hank Tomlin, was trying on a pair of boots when the men by the door stepped farther into the room.

"Everybody just stand there; right there!" The ban- dit's voice crackled with ultimate authority as he pointed his gun at Clyde Carrigan. "You . . . you put that money in a bag!"

The four, more surprised than afraid for the first moments, stared half-believing at the gunmen.

Hank Tomlin, grunting, leaned forward and began pulling on his boot. Instantly the sharp crack of a sixgun cut into the room. But the fat man's movement, which had triggered the shot, also saved him. The bullet hit the boot heel, knocking the boot out of his hand, and was deflected, missing him by a whisker.

Out in the street the shot attracted minor attention. Rock Creek was a cattle and mining town and used to violence, what with the drinking miners and cowboys from the nearby ranches, plus the gamblers, whores, riff-raff element in general, and even now and again a few respectable citizens who attended the drinking establishments and the cribs.

Even so, curiosity is a strong element in humans, and across the street from the General Store a second-story window shot up. Framed by the yellow light of a coal-oil lamp was the head of a man.

Instantly one of the men on the boardwalk outside the store fired.

The man at the window screamed, grabbed his face, writhed for a moment, then toppled out, landing with a thump in the street below

The two gunmen inside the store stood near the front with their weapons trained on the startled group. One of them now walked toward the rear of the building.

Clyde Carrigan had risen from his chair. He stood with his hands shoulder high. His long face was very white. He was a bony man in his seventies with his flesh lying in wrinkles around his eyes, his chin and neck, the knuckles on his long hands.

"Listen, you men . . . don't you realize . . ."

"Shut your mouth!" snapped the man holding the gun on him. "And open that safe!"

Carrigan's breath began to come in little bursts as he bent to the task and finally opened the safe. With the gun only inches from his head he removed the safe's contents. The day's cash was still on the table where he had been working, but there was a lot more in the safe. There were also some trays of jewelry, valuable enough to be locked up for the night. Rock Creek was a boom town, and the men who made the money in the mines didn't mind spending it on fancy gold watches and other flashy items.

The gunman brightened noticeably when Carrigan brought out one of the trays. With his left hand he lifted three or four watches to look at them. Quickly he selected one and told the store owner to wrap the others in a bundle.

The bandit at the door was getting impatient. "For Christ's sake, let's move!"

"Easy," his companion said.

Meanwhile the shot outside in the street and the man falling from the window had brought the town to life. Jason Toohey, a respected businessman, had started hurrying toward Carrigan's General Store at the sound of the second shot. When he was only a short distance away one of the gunmen fired at him, the bullet ricocheting off a blacksmith's anvil at Toohey's right. Toohey was unarmed.

"Hey!" he yelled, fearful and curious at the same time.

A second bullet sang off a rock at his feet and whined on into space. Toohey looked around frantically; he'd lost his hat, but he probably hadn't noticed that detail. Across the street was a saloon, light showing above and beneath its swinging doors. Toohey raced toward it.

The bandit shot again.

Toohey didn't slow down until he was at the edge of the boardwalk. Then he dove forward. His body struck both doors, breaking one and flinging the other wide. Perhaps he saw the astonished faces staring at him from inside the saloon. In the next instant, he was lying face down, shot dead center through the back.

A little distance up the street Mrs. Angela Beanie heard the shooting. She ran outside, curious, and fearful lest her children were in the vicinity.

All at once she gave a choking cry. She had been shot in the chest and killed on the spot.

Meanwhile the bandits inside Carrigan's had collected two canvas bags of money and another filled with precious gold nuggets and dust, besides a good bit of jewelry.

Up the street Corliss Himes, a deputy sheriff, and Joseph Mossman grabbed their guns and ran toward the Carrigan store.

Seeing them, the three gunmen waiting outside the store opened fire. Deputy Corliss Himes fired his gun as he ran, but suddenly staggered.

"Corliss, are you hurt?" Mossman yelled.

Himes was hurt badly. He was weaving about the street, yet still running. Later it was said that the brave sheriff died on his feet as he ran toward the gunmen.

At this point J. A. Nolly, a lawyer, rushed out of his house with his rifle in hand. One of the gunmen fired at his dark form, wounding him fatally.

Fortunately nobody else was hurt, but as the bandits spurred away they shot up the town in the traditional manner, wounding the spotted dog with the chewed ear and scaring a pig nearly to its death. When they finally disappeared it was as if a cyclone had struck.

There on the boardwalk in front of Carrigan's General Store lay five bodies, side by side. Among them was a woman. All had been shot without cause. And somebody pointed out that one was an officer of the law.

But as one sour oldtimer replied when this information was voiced, "Hell, Corliss ain't no more dead than them four others."

Any man living the kind of life John Slocum did would naturally take to the high ground so that he could check his back trail thoroughly. And this was just what that man was doing as he kept the little dun horse in the lee of the big rocks, while they picked their way slowly through scrub oak, spruce, pine, and fir. Both horse and man were well protected from anyone chancing to look up from the deep valley below.

The trail was thin and hard, and the horse made very little sound, clearly aware of the caution with which his rider was concerned.

But Slocum was puzzled and, bending slightly now to spit over his horse's head as the trail took a downward turn, he felt the letter in his shirt pocket pushing into him. Jeremy's letter had caught up with him down at Big Basin only by sheer luck. It had already taken a good while to get to him from the Wind Water country.

"A funny request, John," his old friend had written. "But Dora is going to be all alone out here. I'm asking you to come and help her. There will be money in your name at the bank in Rock Creek. I know it's an awful lot to ask, but she's got no mother any more, and I got that feeling Billy's boys are going to get me. They been after me, and it ain't getting any better. Just to help her get on her feet, or even get her out of the country..."

.

Slocum hadn't been in the Wind Water country in a good while, but he would never forget Jeremy Patches. The man wasn't one to ask for help unless he was about at the end of his rope, and it wouldn't be for himself, Slocum knew. It was obviously for his daughter. So it had to be bad.

He hadn't hesitated. He owed Jeremy, and he was glad to be able to pay something back.

They had rounded a tight bend in the trail and were approaching a grove of cottonwood trees when he caught the shudder running through his horse. The dun snorted, his shoulder muscles rippled, his ears stuck out sideways, then forward, as his gait slowed.

Now the trail opened into the clearing in the cottonwoods, and suddenly he saw the legs. Something caught at his guts. The body was hanging from the big cottonwood that dominated the enclosure. Obviously it had been there for some time. There were several other remains hanging from the same tree, and even from the same branch. Yet, judging by the condition of what was left of the bodies, it had not been a mass hanging. And then, as the stench hit him again, he saw the sign pinned to the tattered coat of the latest body: COURTESY THE SOCIETY FOR THE DISCOURAGEMENT OF HORSE THIEVING.

More than a dozen weather-browned ropes were dangling from other branches, the empty nooses swaying menacingly in the summer breeze. Slocum looked at the bare and naked limbs of the huge old tree reaching toward the clouds like fingers, and remembered Quantrill and the war in Kansas.

As he drew closer the stench was even more terrible, and he had to kick the dun to get nearer to the tree. The bones of other men lay scattered beneath the tree where they had fallen after their flesh had been picked away by the buzzards and prairie wolves. Bits of tattered clothing seemed to be rustling gently as the wind stirred among the bones, skulls, and heavy stench.

Slocum had no wish to dismount, nor even to remain by that well-used cottonwood. Yet something held him. Leaning out of his saddle, he studied the hoofprints under the big tree. It didn't take him long to figure how the hangings had taken place. It had to be vigilantes; the sign surely supported that. But the point was that the hangings were clearly of a particularly cruel form.

The accused would more than likely have been beaten, then tied to a horse with the noose around his neck and his hands secured behind his back. The noose would fit snugly around the unfortunate's neck, the knot under his left ear; the other end of the rope secured to the big branch about twenty feet above the ground.

Then the signal would be given and the vigilantes would ride off. At this point the horse thief's disbelief would hit him, for he'd been waiting for his captors to whip the horse from under him; and indeed he'd conditioned himself for the snap at the end of the rope which would take his life.

But he would soon realize the grim fate they'd prepared for him. They had simply left him to stare his own death in the face and wait. . . .

How long the victim lived depended on the temperament of the horse. The minutes would pass slowly. The man would hear the squawking of the buzzards and he would smell the decayed flesh of horse thieves who had died before him in similar fashion. He'd perhaps think of kicking the horse forward and ending it quickly, but something would stop him. There was always the chance of a miracle.

Slocum realized it fully. He'd heard of such punishment, though he'd never actually run into it before. He could well imagine the broiling sun beating down upon the man as he sat tensely waiting any movement of the horse beneath him. Then night would come and he'd listen to the buzzards and wolves around him. Then it would be day again.

Finally the problem would be solved for him, as it had been for those who went before him. Hunger and thirst would finally force the horse to abandon the weight on its back. As the animal would start to walk, the man would slide off the saddle into space, slowly strangling at the end of the rope.

Slocum took another grim look around. He lighted a quirly to take some of the stench out of his nostrils, and then he turned the dun back down the trail. He told himself that he'd seen enough of the sights for that day.

2

This year the snow again stayed all summer long in the high mountains. The great white shoulders of the Absarokas were dazzling against the infinite blue sky. And then, along the sides of the mountains, in the long green valleys, cattle grazed; cattle from Texas, new to this part of the country, filling themselves on the lush grass. The land was rich with movement. In the meadows and tall timber there was plenty of game. The days and nights were always new, the air crisp as a minted coin. For John Slocum there was no place like it. No place anywhere. Not even back in Georgia. He was glad to be back in the Wind Water country.

Tall and lean, broad-shouldered, Slocum was swift as silk with those big hands, those green eyes that could freeze a man and disarm a woman. People said he had to have Indian blood; they noted his grace of movement, his total alertness even when he was supposedly relaxed.

It was late afternoon when he reached the bridge that crossed the Wind Water River and met the trail coming down from Jeremy's place. Jeremy Patches's place had been, and maybe still was, the highest outfit in that country. It was the same old bridge, repaired some, he could see, that Jeremy had built with spruce limbs and logs laid on the triangular log pilings that were filled with rocks, and tied by rope to trees along the banks.

It didn't look too safe now, though it was still connected to the pilings and cottonwoods. While the dun drank at the river bank, Slocum's eyes searched up toward Jack Creek. The JP outfit had always been invisible until you were right on top of it. But he knew what to look for; the north corner of the corral, only seeing it because he knew it was there.

Slocum touched his boot heel to the dun's belly and they started over the bridge. It was shaky going. Twice the dun spooked at something and for a second or two Slocum thought they'd be hitting the water, but they made it.

They started up the long, winding trail on the other side of the river. A jackrabbit broke from cover and Slocum swung clean around in his stock saddle to look back at the bridge. Nothing moving on his back trail. What was it then? Why did he have that sudden feeling? He faced up the trail again. It wouldn't be long now. There was still no sign of life coming from Jeremy's place.

The sun was almost right down to the rimrocks high above him as he rode to the spring and dismounted. Using his Stetson hat for a dipper, he drank the pure, delicious water. It had been a while since he'd taken a drink from that spring. A good while since he'd busted horses with Jeremy. It had been a good time then, and he'd learned a lot. He wondered if Jeremy's outfit had changed much in the intervening years. He wondered how he'd find Jeremy.

Just when he mounted up a wind stirred, bringing the acrid smell to him, and he felt something tighten inside himself. The dun began to snort and high-step a little, not liking it.

He rode the dun warily the rest of the way to the ranch. And he knew what he was going to find, as the smell of burned timber grew stronger.

At dusk he made his bed beneath the tall trees a good distance from the ranch, picking a place where the smell of charred timber wouldn't be so strong.

It had been grim going through the smashed and burnt buildings, the total destruction, looking for any bodies. Thank God, there had been none. He'd been fearful the whole time of his search that he would come upon the remains of Jeremy or his daughter.

Simply, there was nothing there. Not a building, not a corral standing, only a few random posts, one of which he had seen from below when he'd been at the bridge. He wondered whether the men who had fired the place had deliberately left that post, knowing it was the only part of the ranch visible from the river, and so might delay discovery. It would mean that whoever set the fire knew the ranch well.

The dun didn't like crossing the burnt ground, but Slocum made him walk into the enclosure where the round horse corral had been, the corral where years ago he and Jeremy had driven in the wild horses, roped them, and broken them. It seemed a longer time ago than it actually was.

Now, lying on his bedding, he thought about Jeremy, and wondered idly how old his daughter could be. He remembered the young, grey-eyed girl, just into her teens, helping Grace, her mother, around the place. Jeremy hadn't mentioned in his letter what had happened to Grace.

In the morning he was up early. He had awakened with an immediacy that carried the sense of something not right. Alert, he listened. Only the call of a jay. In one swift movement he was up on his feet, listening.

Dawn was slipping into the sky and he could discern the dun horse only a few yards away where he had picketed him. He watched the animal now. The dun was not feeding on the tasty buffalo grass at his feet, but was standing alert, ears forward. Slocum watched those ears as they moved, and in a moment he moved quickly into the trees and back down the side of the trail up which he had ridden the day before, carefully keeping well out of sight.

It didn't take him long to find the man who had cut his trail. He was just below the spring where he and the dun had stopped to drink; a small, wiry man tightening the cinch on a hammerhead sorrel horse when Slocum stepped up behind him.

"What can I do for you, mister?" Slocum said it softly, but it penetrated all the more for that. He was holding his Colt .44 in his hand.

"Can I turn round?"

"Slow. And with your hands out in front."

It was now that Slocum saw he had flushed a lawman. But he didn't lower his weapon. All kinds of people wore the law on their shirts.

"I asked a question," he said. "Maybe you are wearing the law on that shirt, but what the hell do you think you're doing on my trail?"

"I ain't." He was a dry, dusty man in his early forties, with large wrist bones and knuckles. He looked to Slocum like a man who could move fast.

Slocum didn't tell the lawman he was lying; only the hammer of his sixgun clicked as he drew it back with his thumb.

"So then," the other man said. "I was trailin' you. No point denying it."

"Why?"

"On account of you're John Slocum. And listen, mister. You are standing there pointing a gun at the law."

"I am asking you again why you're following me."

"Suspicion. Folks here got their troubles and when the likes of John Slocum rides into the country I know he ain't just callin' on his Aunt Matilda." He nodded in accompaniment to his own words. "Yep. That is what I am doing."

"That's bullshit!"

"No it ain't. And you be still standin' there with a gun on the law, Slocum."

"I want to know why you're after me," Slocum said.

"I'll tell you. I'll tell you when you tell me where I kin locate Jeremy Patches."

"You mean you don't know?"

"I wouldn't be askin' you if I did, Goddamn it!"

"Why do you want Jeremy?"

He reached up slowly and tapped his shirt pocket with his long thumb. "I got it right here in this flyer; horse thiefing."

"Mister, you got something real wrong. Jeremy

Patches never stole a horse in his life, and I know that by God for a fact! Hell, anybody can print one of those flyers."

The lawman was shaking his head even before Slocum had finished speaking.

He was still shaking his head as the shot rang out and Slocum saw him slump forward, and then drop like a stone to the ground.

"Don't move," the grainy voice said behind him. "Now, first thing, drop yer gun, then second, turn real slow. I am saying—slow!"

The man had emerged from the line of trees just behind Slocum. He was short, with a drooping mustache and deep gutters running down his leathery cheeks. He was old. He looked even to be in his eighties, though he was not at all aged in the way he moved.

"Kick it over. The gun. Easy. Real easy, like." The voice purred, the pale blue eyes were smiling. But not the face. The face was stony. The thick yellow and grey mustache beneath the long, bony nose curved down like horns framing the mouth and big chin, which kept up a slight chewing movement even when the old man wasn't talking.

Slocum was getting angry, but he controlled himself quickly. Somehow he'd been set up, and he wanted to know why. Without even a glance at the man holding the gun on him, he stepped over to the fallen lawman and knelt down to take a look. The bullet had gone right through his heart.

"Dead, ain't he?"

Slocum rose and faced the old man, who was chuckling, his face reddening behind the drooping mustache.

"What's so damn funny?" snapped Slocum. "And why are you pointing that hogleg at me?"

"John Slocum it is! The great John Slocum!" A lump of laughter popped out of his rounded mouth, and he stared at Slocum with his blue eyes big and round. "Not so great now, however, I'd say. Trimmed down a mite, wouldn't you say, young feller?" As he spoke, the laughter was stirring in his face and now he coughed it out in a bark. "Had a hankering to meet you one day; figured as how if I lived long enough I sure enough would! Name here is Dime. Bill. Some folks call me Mysterious Billy. Been expectin' you, Slocum."

"Tell me what you want."

"Well, now, like that there dead feller was sayin' about your friend Patches 'fore he got interrupted, you're wanted for horse thieving. Oh . . . uh . . . you'll get a fair trial. Just like Jeremy Patches when we catch up with him, which we surely will do."

"What horse, and whose is it that I'm supposed to have stolen?" Slocum demanded coldly.

The blue eyes were again big and round, as though the old man was explaining something to a child. "Why, why, that there dun hoss, the one you bin riding." All at once the old man's mood changed. He became brisk, all business. "Anyway, you can expect a fair trial, like I said. You can tell your story to the jury."

"What jury?"

"Why, the jury of the Society of the Discouragement of Horse Thieving."

Slocum heard the other men coming up behind him then. One was leading the dun. In the next moment, he was ordered to mount the horse. There were half a dozen men present now, all of them heavily armed.

"I didn't steal any horse, and you know it," Slocum said, standing firmly and ignoring the order to mount up.

A grin worked its way into Mysterious Billy Dime's face now. A sign ran through his small body. His grin widened and his mouth opened wide with good humor. Slocum noticed that he had a front tooth missing.

"Well, we can always fall back on the other charge agin you."

"Which is?"

Mysterious Billy nodded toward the corpse on the ground. "Murder. And a lawman to boot. Tsk, tsk."

Slocum had his eyes on the old man, and at the same time he was fully aware of the half dozen gunmen easing in around him.

Mysterious Billy was grinning, his lips curled back, showing his teeth. "You sure can't outdraw the lot of us, Mr. Slocum," he said.

"No, but I can kill you."

"Heh-heh. Mebbe. Mebbe. But we don't have to go gettin' ourselves all puckered up, now do we. I mean, we kin talk to this thing; this here unfortunate incident, if you don't mind me usin' some fancy English words here."

"Why don't you get to the point," Slocum snapped. "No, I can't kill the lot of you, but I'll get you and a couple of others, and I'll be careful to kill you where it hurts."

The grin had left Mysterious Billy's face. "Guess you know you are talking to the outfit that has had to take the law into its own hands on account of the regular law being not worth a cup full of cold piss."

"Get to the point. What do you want?" He half turned his head. "And you men there, don't get behind me. I want you in my sights."

"We can take him, Bill," one of the men said.

"No. No, we will not take him. Not now." Mysterious Billy Dime's grin had returned to his ancient face. "Sure . . . !" He held up his hand to stop any argument from Slocum. "Sure, we can trade. I know you're real fast. Friend of mine seen you once in Fort Worth. Said you was lightning. Not *like* lightning; but you *was* lightning. And by God, I do believe it!" He nodded his head slowly, his wide-open, pale blue eyes looking like marbles, and, raising his voice, said, "Now boys, we're all gonna take it easy, hear! And I am going to tell Mr. Slocum here just how it is going to be." He sniffed, cleared his throat, and spat vigorously at the ground.

A moment of silence fell then. And it was Mysterious Billy who broke in.

"I knowed you been an old sidekick of Patches so when we heard you was in the country we figured you come back to see him. Well, you ain't going to see him so easy. On account of he is on the run. About a week ago five men shot up the town—Rock Creek—killed five citizens, including a woman and a sheriff, deputy leastways he was. And they hightailed it. One of them, likely the leader, was Jeremy Patches."

"Can you prove that?"

"Don't have to. Half a dozen men seen him." He sniffed, and spat indolently in the direction of a large stone lying near his feet.

"You're lying."

He watched his words cut into the old man. But the old man, savage for an instant, retrieved the moment and his face settled as he shrugged. "We will settle that one later. For now, get this. Patches, he has been owlhooting in this country since this long time, and he has made some juicy hauls. Us vigilantes are aiming to catch him and stretch him once and for all. Now I *know* you have come back here to locate your old pal. Least, I know you'll be fixin' to locate him. And that's good enough for me and my boys. So, you keep yourself clean, Slocum." He spat, nodded toward the corpse. "We'll let this here serve like a warning. See? For now. I am lettin' you go. But we will have an eye on you. This ain't no place for a nice young feller like yourself." And he was grinning again.

Slocum didn't like it. It was too slick. His eyes were covering the entire group as Mysterious Billy turned, and nodding to his men, mounted the big bay horse someone had led out of the trees.

They were all heading quickly for their horses, and in only moments had ridden off. They rode off quickly, while Slocum listened to the departing hoofbeats. And now he stood looking down at the dead lawman. There was no surprise as to why they had let him go. Obviously, they were hard put to find Jeremy. So they would stick close to him and let him do their work for them.

Well, Jeremy was in a real tight. And with this bunch after him, his old friend was going to need big help.

Slocum's own position wasn't so sweet. Dime and his gunmen would be watching his every move with their gun hands itching, whether he located Jeremy Patches or not. A tougher, meaner, more rotten-looking bunch of saddle rats he hadn't seen since the days of Quantrill and Bloody Bill Anderson. He knew them, their kind. He knew them all the way. And he knew especially well the likes of Mysterious Billy Dime: whip-smart, tricky as a coyote, deadly. The kind, as that oldtimer Snake River Jim used to say, that drank a pint of snake poison every morning for breakfast.

His thoughts turned to the hanging tree with the rotted bodies, picked bones, and remains of rope. Some of the ropes, he'd noted, had been recent; so the vigilante action was still being pressed strongly.

He told himself he should report the lawman's killing. Except that if he did he would lay himself open for questions. At least he should bury the man. But if he did that, he'd never be found.

He settled it by digging a shallow grave, covering it with rocks to protect the dead man from coyotes and wolves, yet leaving enough clear sign about so that anyone looking for the man would find him.

Then, after carefully removing any sign of his own self and the dun horse, he mounted up and rode off.

Many western towns kept a division, or deadline, as it was often called, separating the respectable section of town from the more lively, looser area which offered a quite different version of life and human need. Here, the whores, gamblers, con men, cowboys looking for a good time, and other suspicious transients released their various energies around the clock.

Rock Creek was no exception. Indeed, the deadline was even more marked than in many other towns of a similar size. Rock Creek's respectable citizens were rigorous in their code of behavior. The rules were observed, the letter of the law was upheld. But the men—and, it must be suspected, even some of the women who lived in the "upper" half of the town— were no strangers to random feelings and even overt activities. Rock Creek, everyone avowed, was a respectable town—on the surface. But who could turn a blind eye—and surely not two blind eyes—to the miners, cowboys, card mechanics, and soiled doves who were clearly in view, deadline or no. And the slaughter of the five innocents by the gang that had invaded Carrigan's store certainly emphasized the fact that there was no way of avoiding evil.

Preacher Tom Thompson said so. There was, in fact, seldom a moment when he was *not* saying so. Preacher Tom brought the Word wherever he went throughout the West. He also brought a generous supply of Preacher Tom's All-Over Cure-All, which he sold for a quarter— "payable to the Good Lord for helping us in our need." The fancy label on the flat, easy-to-pocket bottle of All-Over Cure-All stated that "This fabulous elixir will not hesitate to cure consumption, asthma, decline, night sweats, wasting of the flesh, whooping cough and colds, cholera, burns, ringworm, swelled joints, frosted feet, boils, and indigestion; guaranteed to restore ebbing sexual powers in either male or female; efficacious for any venereal disease the buyer might happen to have."

A further claim on the same label put it this way: "And let me say that the knowledge that created this Grand Elixir is second only to CHRISTIANITY in the benefits it is capable of conferring upon mankind."

Thus, it was with "higher authority" that Preacher Tom dealt the cards at the round baize-top table in one of the rooms at the Palace de Joy. The players were earnest as they hunched over their cards, while a small collection of hangers-on stood about, watching the play.

The game was the popular jacks or better. The action was brisk. John Slocum was enjoying himself. He had slipped into town easily that afternoon. No one in Rock Creek had taken more than a look at him. He was not a man you stared at, and this was always evident at a glance. He'd bathed, shaved, put on fresh clothing, and then crossed from the barber/bath to Teddy's Palace de Joy; the name itself intrigued him, not to mention the lively music bursting through those swinging doors, and presently the quality of one or two of the girls he spotted in the barroom. One in particular, sitting on the knee of an enormous bearded man who could only have been a miner, had given him an appraising once-over; and, as he felt the stirring in his trousers, he'd marked her down for the very near future. Meanwhile, he had decided to loosen up with the sociability of a card game.

Among the players besides Preacher Tom and Slocum were a couple of whiskey train operators, who were relaxing from their arduous work of running whiskey into the Indian reservation without being caught by the United States Army at nearby Fort McScott. The other players included a miner, with a black mustache that ran from his upper lip up the sides of his face to his sideburns, a young cowboy with a large wart on his chin, and an extraordinary individual whose face appeared to be a network of wrinkles carved in alligator hide, out of which peered a pair of black, thoroughly malevolent eyes, cold and hard as stones. This person was smoking a short, thick, foul-smelling cigar.

"Teddy, I'll see ya," one of the whiskey train operators was saying, and he pushed forward some chips.

"It is hot as a whore's ass on Saturday night in this room. Shit, one of you open the goddamn door!" The words were spoken with no expression at all. The voice was high and gravelly, but with full authority in it, as a tiny, wrinkled hand simply felt the backs of the cards lying next to the large pile of chips, which bore testimony to the player's skill.

High-Queen Teddy, or Theodora Cadogan, to use the name with which the lady had been born, pushed a stack of chips toward the center of the table. The black eyes rose from the chips to coldly regard the whiskey train man. A forefinger lying on top of her face-down cards flicked to indicate the play was on. With no expression on her face Teddy pulled in her winnings.

It was Preacher Tom's deal. Acknowledging the fact with a beatific smile, he released a reverent sigh, and leaned his pinpoint elbows on the tabletop. Expertly he shuffled, cut, dealt with clean, swift strokes, his glassy eyes looking at each player as he offered the cards. Then he returned to his easy posture, back against the chair, brows raised as he studied his hand, his lids half-lowered in contemplation.

"Would that one might be penny-wise rather than pound-foolish," he intoned.

"Preacher, you are a asshole; there just ain't no way around it!" High-Queen Teddy's face was as impassive as a monument as she said those words.

Preacher was swift with his rejoinder. "If I wasn't a preacher man, High-Queen, I'd be after you faster'n a cat tryin' to climb a greased pole!"

This brought a brisk round of chuckling from the table, plus an obscenity from High-Queen Teddy.

Slocum, smiling inside, kept his face impassive to the table. In this country a smile at the wrong moment could get you dead as quick as a frown. And anyway, he was enjoying himself quietly. He'd picked up some tidbits of gossip, and at the same time he was warming to thoughts of the girl he'd spotted on the way in.

For a time the game slowed. After a few hands Preacher Tom and Slocum had both slightly increased their chips, while the others hadn't lost too much. High-Queen was ahead, but had been playing a closer game on the last few hands.

Teddy reached for a fresh deck. Slocum had been thinking of dropping out, but something in the way she reached for the cards told him the hit was coming now, and he decided to stay in the game.

"Ante a dollar," Teddy said, clamping down hard on her cold cigar.

Nobody said nay to this and the money was dropped into the pot.

"Pass," one of the whiskey train men said, belching at his cards.

High-Queen Teddy struck a wooden lucifer one-handed on her thumbnail, and relighted her cigar.

One of the whiskey train men opened. "Make it a dollar for start."

"Looks like I am in," the miner with the fancy mustache said, and he took a drink from his glass of whiskey.

Teddy dropped her eyes to the backs of her cards and chewed her cigar.

Slocum tossed in a silver cartwheel.

"Dealer stays." High-Queen Teddy's eyes were lidded, waiting.

Slocum had heard of Teddy, one of the toughest gamblers around, who could strip a room full of card mechanics without batting an eye.

Preacher Tom pushed a dollar toward the pot and took two cards.

A wry grin appeared on the mustached miner's face. "One card," he said. "And by God, let it be a good one."

"It'll be what it is," High-Queen said, speaking as though carving the words in stone.

"Three," Slocum said, and for a moment his eyes met Teddy's loaded orbs.

One of the whiskey men released a sigh as he examined his cards. "I should oughta pass, but we'll see, we'll have to see, by God."

High-Queen took the cigar out of her mouth, flicked away a piece of tobacco with her tongue, and said, "Separate the men from the boys, huh? Shit, there ain't a man in the whole of this here town, or God knows where else, what knows what he's doin'!" She paused, puffing on her cigar, her eyes on Slocum. "'Ceptin' maybe this stranger here." And she sniffed, honoring the moment by removing the cigar from her mouth again.

"Teddy, I love ya!" Slocum said, grinning widely and touching his hat brim with two fingers in salute.

"Wantin' it, are you, you dirty man! Well, by God, you can wait'll yer ast!"

This raised a loud round of applause and laughter from the group, who all gripped their glasses and drank vigorously.

Slocum was the first to recover. "Table stakes," he said. "Good enough. I'll bet five."

One of the whiskey men pushed forward five dollars. "And another five," he said, counting it out in cart-wheels.

The miner grinned all over his face.

"I pass," said the second whiskey train man.

"And another five," the miner said.

High-Queen Teddy's voice was as hard and straight as a ruler. "I call."

The first whiskey man said, "I call your five and raise you five more."

The miner squinted at his cards. "See you, raise you five." He was holding his cards so tightly they curved.

Suddenly High-Queen Teddy said, "I call, and raise the pot another ten dollars."

The miner's jaw dropped.

Slocum grinned quietly at Teddy's shrewd play.

"Damn it!" murmured Preacher Tom. "Shit, falling for that, letting the last bet go by. You have just got to have four of a kind, High-Queen!"

"You could find out, you old buzzard!" snapped Teddy, and broke into a loud laugh.

"Let's have a look-see," Slocum said amiably, knowing he wasn't going to take the pot. And he leaned forward.

"The drinks will be on me, boys," Teddy said as she laid down four queens and an ace and pulled in the final pot.

The players leaned back. Someone sighed. Once again High-Queen Teddy had wiped them out. But they didn't mind too much. They'd all had a good time.

The winner was just reaching for her glass of whiskey when the door leading into the barroom opened and a baldheaded man wearing an apron entered.

"God damn you, knock!" Teddy's head whipped around as her black eyes drilled into the bartender.

"I did knock, Teddy."

"Not loud enough. Next time, you knock so I hear it."

"Right." The bartender, a man wearing brand new red suspenders, stood stock still in front of his employer. Slocum took note of the dots of perspiration on top of his head, which had turned pink under High-Queen's lashing tongue.

"Well, what is it?"

"Couple of visitors out at the bar."

"Send 'em into my office. What're the damn fools doing out at the bar, anyways?"

It was not a question that required an answer.

Slocum had risen and started toward the barroom when High-Queen Teddy's words caught him. "Boys, you can all go out the back door." And for good measure she added, "You too, Mr. Slocum."

It was dark outside the saloon. Slocum knew he could hurry around to the front and come in again, on the chance that he might see who the visitors were, but he also knew there wouldn't be time. High-Queen Teddy was ahead of it. He had heard it in her voice. And yet, it was just that very tone in her voice that led him to suspect who the visitors, or at any rate one of them, might be.

He waited outside under the starry sky while the little group dispersed. Preacher Tom appeared to want to stay and talk with him, but Slocum turned away, as though he was in a hurry to get somewhere, and the other man vanished into the shadows of the town.

When he walked around to the front of the saloon it was easy enough to recognize the big bay horse he'd seen Mysterious Billy Dime riding away on after their encounter over the body of the dead lawman. It was hitched right next to a neat little dappled mare standing in the shafts of a shiny black gig.

3

In the tiny room above the bar in the Palace de Joy, John Slocum rolled off the girl and lay beside her on the very rumpled bed. They had left the coal-oil lamp on with the wick low, and as he lay on his back he watched the shadows thrown on the chipped wallpaper and along the ceiling.

Beside him the girl murmured, pressing closer, letting her thigh rub lightly against his, and now, half turning toward him, her hand touched his chest and her fingers began to work down toward his already rising member. As her fist circled her quarry, which hardened to its absolute capacity, he turned to her, embracing her.

"More," she whispered. "More. I want it all night, all night long." And her last word was drawn out as, mounting her, he drove all the way, her legs falling apart and her heels beginning to dig into his back until at long last together they reached the inexpressible instant of total, final ecstasy.

Again they lay side by side, their bodies singing with sweet exhaustion.

"That's twice," the girl whispered.

"That's a good beginning," he said.

There was a pause and she said, "God, how many more can you handle?"

"I thought you said you wanted it all night."

She snuggled close, her lips in his ear, her fingers playing along his back. "I want to do it as long as you want to do it."

"You'll have to prove that," he said.

This time she rode on top of him, wriggling from side to side and pumping up and down his shaft. This time they came quicker, and when they were through she remained on top of him until his organ had relaxed totally and simply slipped out of her. After a while she rolled off him and they slept.

In the early morning they did it again. When he was getting dressed he asked her name.

"What name do you like?" she asked, surprising him.

He waited a moment, watching her in the morning light that was slipping into the almost bare room. She looked even better, he thought, than she had the night before.

Suddenly he grinned. "How about Ginger?"

Her mouth opened in mock surprise. "Golly, how did you guess?"

"From the quality of your lovemaking," he said easily.

She laughed. Her red hair was down, falling to her bare shoulders, almost down to her upturned breasts, which were firm, smooth with large nipples, reddened a good bit more now from his attention during the night. She had a superb figure. He judged her to be in her early twenties.

"So what's your name, sir?" she asked, pretending coyness, holding her finger to her lips and arching her eyebrows.

"You tell me."

For an instant she hesitated, and he knew something was wrong.

"What's the matter?"

"Your name's John Slocum," she blurted out, yet still maintaining her calm.

"Who told you?"

She dropped her eyes, and one hand reached for something to cover her nakedness.

"Teddy?"

She nodded. "Mr. Slocum . . ."

"Call me John."

"Everybody knows about you."

"What do they know?"

She was looking at him steadily now. "That you are one tough man!"

He grinned. "And what do you know about me?"

"That you're one helluva lover!"

"You want to know anything else?"

"No."

There was no chair in the room, only the bed with the girl lying on it and a washstand. Slocum had been squatting beside the bed the way the cowboys hunkered down when they were talking or just doing nothing; now he shifted his weight, but still stayed in his squat, with his forearms along his thighs.

"You know a man named Jeremy Patches?"

"I've heard that name—it's not usual, such a name —but I don't know where."

"Anything else you can tell me?"

"Yeah."

"What?"

"I'd like to see you again."

Slocum stood up, his hand moving to his pocket.

"No," she said.

He felt something go through him like a little shock. Looking at her, he realized there wasn't a drop of sentimentality in her.

"I'd like to buy you dinner sometime." Then he said, "I mean by that, I'd like to have dinner with you."

The smile burst all over her face. "Fair enough," she said.

"So long, Ginger."

As she let him out the door, she said, "You know, that really is my name."

"Ginger."

There was mischief in her eyes. "Virginia. But I like Ginger better."

"So do I," Slocum said.

The barroom was deserted save for the old swamper who was sleeping on the bar when he went downstairs and out into the first light of day.

It was not yet full daylight when he got down to the livery to pick up the dun horse.

"Anybody come lookin' for me?" he asked the hostler, an old man with a harelip. "I got some friends I'm meetin' up with."

"Nope."

But the man looked away too fast. And the next thing

he knew he was looking into the end of John Slocum's Colt.

"I asked you a question, mister, and I want a straight answer. Now that we've got that settled, we'll start over. Who was it asking about me? I mean—right now!"

The hostler caved in under the gleam in those green eyes and the big gun that he knew would either whip him, shoot him, or both.

"Two men. Dave Smith an' Bud Harrigan. They wuz askin'."

"Who are they? They with Dime?"

The hostler was trying not to show how scared he was, but failing in the effort. "Mister, I believe so, but I ain't certain. Nobody knows who for sure rides with Mysterious Billy. Those be the vigilantes," and he added, "case you didn't know."

"What else did they say? What did they say about me?"

"Said nothin'. Mister, that's the God's honest truth! I swears it!"

Slocum knew he had pushed as far as he could. He was convinced the man was telling the truth. And it confirmed what he had thought: that they were leaving him alone so that he could lead them to Jeremy Patches.

"You know a man named Jeremy Patches?" he asked suddenly.

"Never..." But the man stopped, seeing the movement in Slocum's gun hand. "Not seen him about in this good while, mister. Used to know him. Ran two, three hundred head up on the mountain other side of Jack Creek. But I heard he left the country, something like that."

"You know who fired his outfit?"

"No sir, I do not." The hostler was almost shaking by now, as he felt the full force of Slocum's demand on him. "Mister, I am telling you . . ."

But Slocum had already walked into the barn to get his horse. Five minutes later he was on his way out of town. As he rode down the main street he knew he was being watched. He knew they were that close. Good enough. In fact, it was going to be a lot easier for him knowing that they were that close than thinking they were throwing a wider loop. The question was, would they continue to dog his trail that closely. He hoped they would. It would be easier to shake them.

From the window of an upstairs room in the McCready House, two men watched John Slocum's departing figure.

"He looks like what people say about him," said the taller of the two. This was a man dressed in black, wearing a frock coat, spotless white linen, polished Wellington boots—all in black save for the shirt. There was money in those clothes. Henry Skinner could, of course, afford it. He could afford just about anything.

His companion couldn't have appeared in a more different light. He was ragged, a word that gave Mysterious Billy Dime the least offensive description. The two shared one thing in common, however, and each knew it. This was the lure of excitement and money. Only wealth had eluded Mysterious Billy, whereas Skinner was more than well-to-do. He yet craved more. But mostly Henry Skinner craved power. And Mysterious Billy Dime did too, only in a different way.

"You're telling me he's looking for Patches," Skinner was saying. They had retreated from Skinner's bedroom window and now sat in chairs. There were two in this special room that Skinner kept reserved for the times he stayed overnight in town, his regular home being some miles out of Rock Creek.

"He's an old friend of Patches," Dime said.

"And when they meet up they'll work together, I imagine."

"That is how it reads." Mysterious Billy nodded.

"Then why didn't you get rid of him then and there?"

A gap suddenly appeared in Mysterious Billy's mouth where a front tooth was missing, and Skinner watched the grin spreading.

"On account of we didn't have nary a idee on where in hell to locate Jeremy Patches, and so figgered as how Slocum might lead us to him. Save us the work, and maybe some mistakes."

Henry Skinner was already nodding his round head, which was partially bald, his carefully placed strands of long, silky black hair failing to cover the rather large expanse of freckled flesh. "Of course, Dime. But of course! That is easily seen by your choice of decision. But you are taking a major risk. That man Slocum is no fool. I have heard things about him."

Mysterious Billy's thin upper lip curled in an obvious sneer which was not lost upon the other man. But Henry Skinner said nothing. He found it tiresome dealing with Dime. Everything had to be explained. True, he furnished the brute power that was needed, but he was dumb as an ox's tooth. Henry Skinner suddenly wished he was back in the Cheyenne Club with his acquaintances in the Stockgrowers Association.

But he pulled himself together. There was business at hand, work to be done. And besides, Henry Skinner, while enjoying the seduction of dreams, was also a realist. The Cheyenne men weren't quite his intimates. His foot had entered the Cheyenne Club, even more than once or twice, but he was not by any means secure there. Thus far, that level of power remained beyond him. Someday? Yes. But in reality and for the present it was better to be a big fish in a small pond. Later he could move into higher echelons. One step at a time. There was strategy and tactics, and he was not one to confuse the two necessities. Besides, he had friends in Washington and that was of infinitely greater value.

"Very well," he said now. "Find Patches. He has—I have been well-informed—he has been stealing horses and cattle too. He needs to be brought to justice. If you feel your method with this man Slocum will pay off, then by all means use it." He stood straight in front of Dime. "Don't fail. Do not fail me!"

Mysterious Billy Dime grinned, and nodded his old head, causing his wattles to quiver.

Henry Skinner sat down again and looked toward a corner of the room as though thinking. "Now then, we will take up the business of the whiskey trains."

Mysterious Billy grinned again, wider this time as he reached inside his large coat. His hand came out gripping a bottle filled with brown liquid.

Skinner nodded in approval, a smile touching the corners of his mouth. "Yes, good thing to sample the product. We do not want the redskins, or anyone else for that matter, to receive inferior goods."

Mysterious Billy chuckled. He liked it when Henry talked fancy like that. He didn't always understand it, but it sounded good. And Mysterious Billy was feeling good anyway. There were a lot of people he didn't like, including Henry Skinner, but he had discovered now that he disliked John Slocum more than anybody else he could think of. He didn't know why. It never really occurred to him to ask why. It didn't matter. He knew only that he wanted to kill him.

Slocum reasoned that they would not be expecting him to head for Jeremy's JP a second time, not with the place burned to the ground, not after his encounter with the vigilantes. All the same, he took every precaution, leaving town and heading in the opposite direction from Jeremy's outfit. He left an open trail, easily visible, but not too obviously so. He did make it somewhat difficult to follow, in keeping with a man covering his tracks.

From Rock Creek he rode south until well into the hot forenoon. At Betty Creek he walked the dun horse into a thin stream for a drink, and to let the cool water run over its hocks while both man and animal rested.

Slocum had no idea where to start looking for Jeremy Patches. Any inquiries he'd made in town had drawn forth either ignorance or fear, or both. Although he had learned that Grace Patches had died of pneumonia two years back, he heard nothing about Dora. It was as though Dora and Jeremy had vanished. There was in fact nowhere to begin other than the JP. But what he could possibly discover there he had no idea. He had decided for a start that he would simply try to feel the place. He would put himself in Jeremy's shoes and see what he would do.

When they had rested, he turned the horse upstream and followed the winding creek, staying right in the middle for some distance until a place offered itself where the bank was hard and not likely to leave tracks.

There was a meadow there, but he didn't enter it. He pointed the dun into the trees and dismounted and led the animal around to the other side of the meadow.

Mounting then, he followed an old game trail leading north and west.

That night he camped high up under the rimrocks overlooking Jeremy's ranch and the river that ran far below. The Wind Water ran right through the center of the long valley, all the way down through Rock Creek. Jeremy's was the only ranch this far in the mountains. The only known way to reach the place was up the narrow, steep trail he'd taken the other day. He wondered now if anybody had come looking for the lawman whom he'd buried under the little pile of rocks.

He made a dry camp, no fire, eating some beef jerky he'd brought with him. The night was cool and the smell of pine and spruce was strong. He lay on his bedding, fully clothed, with his Colt and his Winchester right by his hand. He could smell the dun horse, which was picketed just a few feet away.

As he lay there in the clear, clean mountain air he let a part of his attention turn to Jeremy and the events of the past couple of days since he'd run into the vigilante bunch.

Some of the people he'd talked to in town still felt Jeremy Patches hadn't been part of the gang that had shot up Rock Creek and murdered five citizens. But others did believe the rumor and gossip that he had been part of the gang. Why? Slocum had asked the question, but people were afraid to speak up. They turned away. It had been too much of a shock, too bold an event to be easily assimilated. And besides, not many people in town had known Jeremy Patches.

Jeremy had always been a man who kept to himself. He'd built his outfit high up, far away. That was his nature. But Slocum had heard of the fighting with the stockgrowers who were moving into the country. He'd run into that kind of thing before, and he knew how nasty it could be. Was it that? he wondered. Were the big stockmen trying to push the small cattlemen out? Or was it the mines? Had somebody struck a new vein, perhaps close to the JP? Or was someone running a sandy on the whole community; was there maybe a railroad spur coming and so land values were going to shoot way up?

Why was Jeremy Patches a target? He knew Jeremy to be a quiet, though occasionally feisty man who had come out to Wyoming when he was young, and had stayed, loving the land. Slocum remembered well the time he'd stayed with Jeremy and Grace breaking mustangs which they'd run in from the open range. God, it had been fun! Hard work, but fun!

Try as he might, he could think of no reason why Jeremy's outfit would be burned to the ground and Jeremy—and possibly his daughter too—go into hiding. Had they maybe even left the country? This Slocum doubted. Not Jeremy. That man was no easy one to backwater. And besides, Jeremy had written him a letter.

Slocum was not a man to chew anything to pieces. He thought it all through as far as it would go, looking at the possibles and probables, and then he let it go. It would show itself soon enough. All he had to do was keep his eyes open. Especially the eyes in the back of his head.

The smell was still there, though perhaps because he was expecting it this time it didn't seem as strong. Yet the carnage sank into him more deeply. Nothing had been untouched by the fire. The log ranch house, the bunkhouse, the barn were simply charred remains. This time he took a closer look at everything, and still found no signs of any bodies. Yet the firing had been recent.

He hobbled the dun with leather thongs that he carried for the purpose and went slowly over what had been the JP outfit.

It was hot now, with the pale sun directly overhead as he came back down from where the bunkhouse had stood to squat in the remains of the round horse corral. He hunkered, his forearms on his thighs, while with one hand drawing lines in the hard earth with the end of a stub of sagebrush he'd picked up.

He listened. He was sure no one had tracked him, sure that he would hear them up here. On his way up he had checked the place where he had buried the lawman. No one had been there. Only the tracks of a coyote. He remembered the coyote pup Jeremy had trained to become a pet. He'd been just like a dog, following Jeremy, permitting himself to be leashed, until the day when, for no apparent reason, he'd suddenly turned and bitten his master right through his little finger. Jeremy had moved like grease. In one movement he'd slammed the feisty animal onto its back and then tromped its head with the heel of his boot.

Patching up his finger Jeremy had grinned through his pain. "Like Old Coyote Johnnie Wagner used to say, you can't trust the buggers. Sooner or later..." And Jeremy had left the sentence unfinished as he'd walked into the house for the whiskey bottle.

Jeremy Patches was no one to mess with either, Slocum was reflecting. Had he been here when they fired the place? Or had they done it while he was out checking his stock? And where was the JP stock? Run off, he supposed; probably re-branded.

He tried to picture how it could have happened. Jeremy riding in, smelling the fire, feeling the heat of it. Or it could have been night—which was more than likely—and the fire would be lighting up the sky.

Or had he been here when the attackers rode in? Had there been a fight, in the course of which he'd been holed up in one of the buildings and so had invited the firing? But then, how had he escaped?

Slocum had carefully examined what remained of the building logs, searching for bullet holes which would have indicated a gunfight, but there were none. There was no evidence at all that there had been a showdown with guns.

The thought occurred to him suddenly that Jeremy could have fired the ranch himself. But knowing how he felt about the JP, Slocum discounted this notion pretty quickly. Jeremy loved the place. He had built it himself, mostly without help, save for the spell Slocum had stayed with him, when in between running horses and breaking them they'd built the round corral.

He shifted his weight and squinted at the sun. Just past noon. He stood up and walked over to his saddle rigging where he had laid it after stripping the dun, and took out his field glasses. Then, squatting again, but this time facing away from the ranch, facing out to the big rimrocks far across the valley, he looked down at the wide, green and brown land, rolling away below him.

No sign of any riders. A band of elk grazing, some pronghorn antelope bounding across a patch of green, an eagle sailing through the sky. Horses down at the T-Bar, one of the big outfits in that country, he remembered.

Something glinting caught his eye on the other side of the Wind Water. Something moving. A wagon drawn by a team with two riders on saddle horses accompanying it. They were almost hidden by trees along the river and, but for the glint of—gun metal likely—he would have missed them. Now the wagon stopped. The riders got down while the driver of the team stayed where he was on the seat of his wagon box.

Slocum took a moment to sweep the immediate area around the team and wagon, but there was no one else on the scene. However, now someone was approaching on foot from the trees. The men were taking boxes out of the wagon, passing them over the endgate. Now another man had appeared from the trees, and the boxes or crates were being passed to him, and he carried them into the trees. Perhaps there were other men there, or a second wagon to receive the cargo. He was pretty clear on what the crates contained. He wondered if the two whiskey train men he'd played cards with at the Palace de Joy were down there. In any case, it was not an uncommon scene: the whiskey train bringing whiskey to sell illegally to the tribes. Probably the Arapahoes, he decided.

He took another look to see if there was anything moving suspiciously on this side of the river and then, satisfied, he slipped the glasses back into their case.

He stood up and walked back toward the area where the corral had been. He wondered if Jeremy's trouble had anything to do with the whiskey train. He couldn't imagine how. No, it had to be cattle or land rights, or maybe water—any or all of those.

As he stood outside the charred and fallen logs that had been Jeremy's barn and looked up toward the bunk-house, he felt something pulling at him. He was thinking then how the vandals had burned everything, including even the outhouse, which they had also pushed over; a final touch of insolence. Yet there was something he couldn't remember.

At that moment he heard the click of a rifle hammer. His hand started to the Colt at his hip.

"Do not move! I've got you right between the shoulder blades!"

Slocum froze.

"Can I turn around?"

"Slowly. Real slow, and with your hands raised. No—no, first you unbuckle your gunbelt and let it drop to the ground. Then you can turn."

"Good enough. I am doing just what you're telling me." Slowly he unbuckled his gunbelt and let it drop. Then, carefully steppIng out of the belt so his feet wouldn't get tangled if he had to move quickly, he turned, with his hands raised to shoulder height.

"Long time since we saw each other, Dora," he said to the resolute young woman who faced him with her finger on the trigger of the Henry rifle.

He watched the shock come into her face as she began to recognize him.

"It's John Slocum," he said now.

She was nodding a little, as though not believing what she saw. Her face was drained of color. And in the next moment she had put down the rifle, almost dropped it, and taken a step toward him.

He caught her before she fell.

4

Weird echoes struck the rock walls as the train chugged through the narrow canyon. Engineer Cy Tilden had closed his engine cab tight against the night storm he was expecting. Just now he wasn't sure if he heard the sharp crack of a rifle.

He strained his eyes to see better. The engine's headlight was throwing a shimmery halo in the rain that was beating down on the train. Turning, he opened one of the windows and the storm burst into the cab, hitting him in the face. The cracking sound came again and he saw a red spot in the light up ahead.

"Hey!" he yelled at his fireman, Ed Burke. "Sounds like trouble up ahead."

"That ain't thunder 'n' lightnin'," mumbled Burke.

"Sounds like rail torpedoes," Tilden shot back at him, leaning out to get a better look. Quickly he pulled back into the cab and began to brake down as fast as he could.

"Looks like a warning flare up there," shouted Burke, leaning out. "Only a few yards now..."

"Could be a washout," snapped Tilden. "Shit take it!"

The train stopped short and Cy Tilden went to the other window to take a look, squinting into the rain and the glare up ahead from the light. Without realizing what he was doing his hand dropped to his gun.

"Put yer hands up, engineer!" a hard voice shouted. "And you, too, fireman!"

Cy Tilden couldn't see anyone, but without even thinking, his anger overtaking him, he drew and shot at the voice.

The answer came in a hail of bullets. Tilden collapsed onto the window, dead. His fireman crouched down near the firebox, ready to protect himself. But already a masked man had climbed into the cab, and he didn't have a chance.

Meanwhile, immediately behind them in the express car, the expressman and the guard, both well aware of the big shipment of money they were carrying, had heard the shooting. The guard, a man of duty, drew his sidearm and hurried to a place where he could peer out to see what was happening. The glass window was small, and just framed his face. It was enough. His last act on earth was to become the perfect target. He twisted, bent, fell, and died. Two shots had done it, though one would have managed.

The sudden death of the guard—within the space of a mere second—shook the expressman to his core. Yet J. B. Phillips was a brave man and rallied sufficiently to rush to the doors of the car and lock them. His next action was to remove some of the leather bags from the safe. There were many, but he couldn't take them all. The bags weighed a good deal, since they were filled with gold. But there was no place to hide them. Suddenly genius touched him. The pot-bellied stove had a fire in it, which had been lit both to make coffee and also to take off the chill of night, which even in summer came in the high Rockies. Phillips pulled open the stove door and jammed six of the bags into the big stove. His reasoning was sound; melted gold is still gold.

Finding the express door locked, the attackers didn't waste a moment. Someone planted a stick of dynamite under the front of the car and lighted it.

The explosion blew away a whole corner of the car. Immediately, two masked men climbed aboard and covered the expressman, who had protected himself by crouching behind a heavy desk at the far end of the car.

"On yer feet and open the safe!" barked one of the train robbers.

Phillips didn't hesitate. It was clear the robbers were not men of mercy. In less than a few minutes the two outlaws had passed all the leather bags from the safe to their companions outside the train. Then, warning Phillips to make no move to follow, they swung down from the wrecked express car, mounted their waiting horses, and disappeared with their companions into the storm.

It was soon known that the total money in the shipment was $65,000; the gold that had been stuffed into the stove came to about $14,000, and it was not harmed by the heat. What was striking, besides the amount of the loot, was the two killings, the wrecked car, and the bold ruthlessness of the men, who evidently knew their trade well. Moreover, they were lucky. Because of the rain their tracks washed away.

The holdup at Medicine Gap took place around half past ten and it was well after midnight when the acting sheriff of Rock Creek, T. P. Daventry, was notified. Daventry, who had been acting in the capacity of sheriff since the murder of Corliss Himes by the men who had shot up Rock Creek, was no novice. T. P. wasted not a moment on speculation. By dawn he had half a dozen men with good horseflesh ready as a posse. He had also commandeered a special engine and freight car to take them out to the scene of action, nearly thirty-five miles away. By the time they got there the rain had stopped. The heavily armed men led their horses down from the freight car and mounted.

But the rain proved an invaluable ally to the bandits; their tracks had been erased. Hours later the posse returned to Rock Creek, exhausted, discouraged, and still furious.

The town, meanwhile, was just beginning to stir from the shock of the latest robbery and killings.

"Question is, are they the same outfit?" T. P. first asked the wall in his small office on Main Street. Later, he addressed the same question to whoever questioned him on the two affairs. So far, nothing had been discovered about the five who had invaded Carrigan's, shot up Rock Creek, and murdered five citizens.

T. P., taking over even as Rock Creek's former sheriff was being prepared for burial, hadn't missed a beat. He had ridden out with a posse then, but to no avail.

Earnest citizens had finally urged him to contact the vigilantes, but he had refused, stating that as long as there was law in Rock Creek, then the vigilantes were unlawful. If any of them wanted to sign on as deputies, he would more than likely accept them. Otherwise, they were definitely acting on their own; that is, outside the law.

But now, with the dramatic train robbery and the killing of two men, citizens again urged T. P. to call in the vigilantes.

"Wait for the railroad to send someone, you'll wait forever," an irate citizen pointed out. "And I for one figure the train and the five killings here in the main street of Rock Creek was done by one and the same gang of murderers!"

This speech had been addressed to a small group of listeners outside the Magpie Bar and Gambling Establishment. Enoch Williams had delivered it. Enoch was a big man in town, and he carried weight with the citizenry.

Privately, T. P. was tempted. But to the world of Rock Creek his "No!" was as firm as the line of his jutting jaw. T. P. knew very well what would happen if he allowed such a happening, and he said so. The vigilantes would run the town.

"But they have cleaned up the horse-thiefin'!" pointed out one angry rancher. And others had concurred.

T. P. Daventry was wondering what had happened to the stock detective who had come through town and been directed toward the Jeremy Patches outfit up by Jack Creek. He was wondering about a number of other things too, like the firing of the JP, and the ease with which horse thieves and other owlhooters were apprehended by the vigilantes. T. P. was surely no bluenose, but he did not approve of instant justice. Though let it be said that this ropey man, who had to be in his sixties, was not one to be standing around with his hands in his pockets when that moment that cried for "justice"—just, or unjust—came.

He finished building his smoke, licking it and rolling it in his calloused thumb and forefinger. Then, with one swift stroke, he drew a wooden lucifer from his hatband, struck it one-handed on his thumbnail, and touched the flame to his cigarette.

"The hell with it," he said aloud, and wondered where the cat was.

She hadn't fainted, but it had been close, he could see. She stood close to him now, shaking, and holding her hand to her eyes. Slocum waited.

Presently, she looked up, moving a little bit away from him; a gesture to get her bearings.

"I am glad to see you," she said, and her voice was almost a whisper.

"Glad to see you, too," Slocum said.

"Dad's all right," she said then, answering his unspoken question. "He's laid up a bit so he sent me down here."

"Where is he?" Slocum said. "Up at his old hunting cabin?"

"You remembered it. He wondered if you would."

"Only just now."

They had started to walk toward a stand of pine trees and now sat down on a thick bed of brown needles in the shade.

"How did it happen?" Slocum asked, nodding toward the nearest charred logs.

"While we were out checking stock." She fell silent, then added, "I'll tell you about it. In a minute. Like some jawbreaker, would you?"

He grinned at that, liking her spirit, the way she was handling it, the way she was with him.

"I sure would. Haven't had a good cup of coffee since I dunno." He spread his hands apart and shrugged.

Her laughter was more in her eyes than in any sound, though it did come out. "I've got the makings on my saddle," she said.

And she was up on her feet and moving into the trees. He remained where he was, his eyes sweeping down to the land below them, below the lip of the ranch that was the widest part, near where the house had stood. Below, there was a sharp slope which a man could handle, but which was pretty tough business for a horse.

Seeing no sign of any human below, he stood up, scanned again, and then began gathering wood to make a fire for the coffee.

When she came back and began boiling the water in her pot he studied her. She was in her early twenties, with long dark brown hair falling to her shoulders, and grey eyes which seemed to turn up at the outside corners, though he couldn't be certain since he didn't want to embarrass her by staring. Even so, she was a beauty, with a full, firm bust stretching her shirt to its utmost, while her thighs and buttocks filled every stitch of her denim trousers. Everything seemed to match, or complement, everything else. Her wide mouth with full lips was a perfect partner to her turned-up nose. High cheekbones were just right to follow below those eyes and clear forehead. Once, when she turned her head suddenly, he caught the lobe of a delightful ear. And suddenly he realized she knew very well how he was noticing her. And this too was a delight.

She poured his coffee into a tin cup he had brought

from his own pack, and poured her own into a clean white enamel bowl which was smaller than the average mug, but had no handles.

"I like it without handles," she said, and added, "I noticed you looking at my bowl. It belonged to my mother. I like it without handles especially in the winter because it's such a good way to warm my fingers. Don't you think?"

"I'm sure that is so," Slocum said gravely, feeling the pressure of her delightfulness in his loins. "And also the coffee is good."

"Doesn't quite break your jaw, then, does it?" she said, smiling.

"It warms the heart," Slocum said, grinning at her. "I'm glad I finally found you," he went on, letting the implications of the remark fall wherever they would. For while he was glad, as he put it to himself, to find Jeremy's daughter, he was even more glad to find this gorgeous young girl in the fullness of her life.

They were silent for a long moment. Then the girl spoke. "They came while we were out checking brands, as I said. When we rode in they opened fire. One of them hit Dad in the leg. Not a bad wound, but then they hit his horse, and that was serious. When he fell Dad hurt his leg. But we still got away. As luck would have it, Dad had a tough little strawberry roan picketed by the spring, just in case of trouble like this. He was back of the spring, hidden, and we made it there; and we just got out. The fire was out of control. There was nothing we could do. There were too many of them." A sigh ran through her, and her breath caught for a moment. "It was closer than I want to think about."

"Then you hit for the cabin."

"Then we hit for the cabin." She looked away, trying

to cover what she was feeling. "I still don't know how many people—if any—know about the cabin."

"I know about it. That means it can be known about."

"Reckon." She had put her bowl down and was looking out across the valley.

"How come they want your outfit, or want Jeremy, whichever?" Slocum asked. He was finding it terribly hard not to keep his eyes constantly on the girl.

"That's something I don't know. And Dad doesn't either."

"I had a notion at first it might have been cattle. Somebody wanted your water, or access to mountain pasture, something like that. And where's your stock?"

"Scattered." Dora was looking down into her empty coffee bowl. "Dad figures they want to get rid of the small stockmen."

"But has anyone said anything? Anyone offered to buy your place?"

"No. Nothing. Nobody has shown the slightest reason why they would want the JP. Take a look." She opened her hand and made a sweeping gesture with her arm. "The trail up here doesn't go anywhere. There's no gold or silver or anything worth mining up here. All the mines are on the other side of the mountain. The land isn't worth much for anything, not even for cattle. I know that's why Dad got it. Because he wanted a place far away. He and Mom were like that. I can't explain it. Well . . . anyway, you knew them. You were here breaking horses. Although I hardly remember." And then she quickly added, "No, that's not true. Of course I remember; it wasn't that long ago. I guess I'm just talking silly. It's all been so worrisome."

He said nothing, simply watching the side of her

face, the curve in her cheek where it met her high cheekbone.

"You weren't here much, I recollect. You had measles, or something, and your mother took you to her family in Billings."

She nodded in vague agreement, her thoughts evidently on the grim situation at hand, rather than the past.

"We'll go there then?" she said suddenly, standing up. "To the cabin?"

He stood beside her. "No. You go. I'll be along. Tell Jeremy I'll be along."

He watched the surprise come into her face, but she didn't ask him why he wasn't coming. He waited to see if she would. But she knew how to be. He was damn glad to see that, glad she didn't ask why, but took it as it was given.

She gave a little nod of her head, while Slocum could only feel his desire mount.

"I'll be along later," he said.

She said nothing.

"Thanks for the coffee."

"You're welcome."

"I'll be heading into town, I want to see what I can pick up. Anything you or Jeremy need?"

"Some rounds for the Winchester."

"Forty-four-forty," he said.

"Dad can pay you."

"I forgot his Christmas present," Slocum said drily.

The girl smiled at that, her grey eyes twinkling. Slocum felt his heart thumping. For a moment they just stood looking at each other. Finally he felt he couldn't stand it any longer.

"We'll have some coffee hot for you," Dora said suddenly.

"Be sure you keep sharp to your back trail," he told her.

She nodded.

He had walked with her into the trees, following a game trail that opened into a clearing. There was a little sorrel gelding cropping the buffalo grass. He was saddled, and was feeding with the bit in his mouth.

Slocum watched her swinging into the stock saddle, her buttocks tightening every inch of those denim trousers.

After she had ridden away, smiling down at him, he was glad. When she was around it was damn hard to keep his mind on business.

There was something further that Slocum wanted to look into, however, before he did anything else. It had been at the edges of his mind while he'd been talking to the girl, and only now had come in closer.

He had seen something glinting when he had looked down toward the river with the field glasses; earlier, before Dora had appeared. And then he had seen the men unloading the crates. He had reasoned that they were whiskey traders supplying the Indians with whiskey. The glint could have been a rifle. That had put the thought into his head. But of course, there would be bound to be guns present; the whole affair was illegal.

Still, the thought kept at him and he found himself riding down to the place where he'd seen the men and the wagon. He was wondering now if the crates had been carrying guns. The tribes were eager for weapons, not only for hunting but possibly for occasional raids on the local ranches and farms.

Now the sun was hot on his back. He could feel his toes moving in the dampness inside his boots. The heat of his saddle was unbearable to the touch of his bare hand. Sweat was running down the sides of his face and dripping into his eyes.

He examined the horizon ahead and the land below him as he wound down the trail. He took his time, letting his eyes move carefully, studying all the sharp crags and rims across the river, and the sweeping land below. There were no riders about. Still, he did not relax his vigilance.

Above and all around him the sky was completely clear—very light blue directly above him, and seeming to be carrying no air at all. There was no wind, only the movement of heat waves. The dun's shod hooves rang whenever they touched rock.

Halfway down Slocum drew rein at a creek so that the two of them could drink. He felt cooler for the water, and his vision seemed better than it had been in the intense heat. Later, at the river, he drew rein again, and waited; watching not only with his eyes but with his whole self, listening for anything that sounded different and not usual in the environment. Suddenly, the dun pointed his ears. Both he and the horse had spotted something grey in the silver sage up ahead. Easily and smoothly, Slocum pulled the Winchester from its scabbard. Was it a timber wolf?

Only the grey spot didn't move. Then, after a short while studying it, Slocum saw that it was a piece of wood. He put it down to the heat that he'd been fooled like that, but told himself to be a whole lot more careful next time.

He rode on, checking his back trail every so often, while now and then struck by all the color: the green grass, the silver sage, and the tawny-colored slopes leading into the mahogany-colored trees and brush, and then the purple leading up to the great rocks, and the redness of the sheer thrust of those huge rimrocks striking into the pale blue sky. Ahead of him along the river there were blues and yellows of the many, many flowers, mixed in with the olive-colored bullberry bushes and the pale, whitish cottonwoods.

He was wondering, as he rode, if Jeremy's trouble was in fact the cattle. They weren't so far from where the big Wyoming cattle war had taken place. Slocum had known some of the fringes of that grim episode. He knew the big cattlemen still stole from each other consistently, through their hired hands, not facing such a task themselves, and often overran and then acquired everything the small stockman had. It could be simply that with Jeremy's JP.

Whatever the reason, they were a rough bunch with their "regulators," their gunmen. Mysterious Billy Dime was a good example of what he could expect from now on. He knew that type from the War days, back in the time with Quantrill. The Raiders had that look. Especially Quantrill and Bloody Bill Anderson. Crazy, bloodthirsty, senseless. There was only one way to deal with such men. Be faster!

He was right next to the river now, and at a shallow place he crossed.

Now he was in the meadow where he'd spotted the wagon. It was a fairly large area of grass, level, rich, and moist, the kind of place, Slocum told himself, where a man could close-pasture his horse overnight and know that in the morning the animal would be fat and tangy and ready for a day's hard work. But now the meadow hadn't been grazed in a good while, for it was thick with dandelion, sourdock, evening star; too many flowers for a man to count. He let the dun have his head for a moment to feast, while he sat still in his saddle, breathing in the aromatic hay.

Suddenly he spotted the wagon tracks, and he climbed down from the horse. There were horse droppings, the marks of shod hooves. And then—right here —just what he'd begun to suspect. Someone had dropped a cartridge. It was unfired. It had to be ammunition for a Spencer repeater. Just what any ornery Indian would give his soul for, Slocum told himself. So it was indeed guns. Near the cartridge he found some wood splinters, and the grass still bent from where a crate had been placed and evidently opened.

He found the empty crate about a hundred yards into the stand of box elders. Yes. It had to be Spencers, the new repeating rifles that even much of the army of the West hadn't yet been issued, but which private persons were selling to the tribes.

Only a few feet away he came upon a scattered deck of playing cards which, on close examination, he found to be marked. Somebody, clearly, had come out second best. He wondered if it had been Indians. He knew many Indians loved to gamble, and were slick as most whites at straight playing or cheating. But whether it had been a red man or a white using the marked deck he couldn't figure out. It was simply clear that a transaction had been made, and he was sure—especially after finding an empty whiskey bottle—that it had been for both liquor and guns. That for sure did not bode well for any of the ranchers in that particular part of the country.

As he rode away, he tried to remember anything he might have heard about Indian trouble, but there had been nothing. The Arapaho, who were more numerous than any other tribe around the Wind Water country, had been notably peaceful, sticking close to their reservation. If there'd been even a rumble of trouble he would have heard about it in Rock Creek. News such as an Indian flareup traveled fast.

Not sure if this speculation had anything at all to do with the trouble Jeremy was having, he was undecided whether or not to follow the wagon tracks. He decided to follow at least for a little way, for he wanted to see where the accompanying tracks of unshod ponies would split off at some point from the wagon and the whites' shod horses.

Henry Skinner was a man of method and habit, who, seeing a goal, allowed nothing in the whole world to stand in his way to attainment. Someone had once said that Skinner was a man as thin as a broomstick, as cheerful as a tombstone, and as deadly as a gallon of snake poison. He had other qualities: he knew banking, real estate, mining, business of all kinds from front to back and inside out. And there were those who claimed he was so devilishly efficient and thus successful because the man simply had been born and had lived for more than sixty years without a heart.

The girl Ginger would never have disagreed with such a summation of Skinner's character, but she was a girl who also knew her business, the first tenet of which was that the customer must have his way. And so she let Henry have his. The only thing she couldn't understand was why the "skinny little wretch," as High-Queen Teddy called him behind his back—though worse to his face—had chosen her, Ginger, for his companion. The point was that he paid well. Neither Henry nor Ginger could be called stupid, therefore.

At the moment the pair were lying side by side on Ginger's bed in the Palace de Joy, with a thin film of sweat covering their naked bodies.

"That was delightful, my dear," Skinner said after a long silence, during which neither slept but each was occupied with thoughts.

"Yeah . . ." the girl allowed, wondering if the man beside her would ever live long enough to say something different than those words after having had her. Every single time it was exactly the same, she was thinking. Now, by golly, he'll say he wants a drink of water.

"I could use a drink of water," Skinner said.

She bit her lower lip. Word for word. What next? Oh yes, something about taking a leak. How did he put it?

"I believe I should relieve myself, my dear. I'll be right back."

When he was gone, she got up and began dressing, and was suddenly struck dumb at a realization that appeared like a bolt of lightning. For indeed, she had risen from the same side of the bed as always with Henry, had stretched, looked at herself in the mirror on top of her dresser, scratched her right buttock, and then sat down and pulled on her left stocking, then her right, in that order. Just the same as always!

She had a smile on her face when Skinner came back into the room. And a prank had started in her.

"Henry!"

"You've never called me that before!" he snapped.

"I am calling you that now, Henry my dear." And she swept to her feet as he sat down. She stood with her back to him, totally bare, bumping her behind from side to side, and then turned to face him with a big grin on her face. The sour Henry Skinner was delighted, his pasty face suddenly russet with the rush of excitement, and he felt his loins heating up.

"I believe, my dear, that we should perhaps not hurry. Waste, after all, has always been the enemy of distinction."

"Henry, I dunno what you're talking about." She stood with her hands on her hips, pretending aggression, a mock-tough look on her face, while his eyes bored into her damp red bush.

"Lie down, and prepare yourself to receive," he said.

And as they both fell onto the bed, they both began to choke with laughter. But not for long; only for a moment, prior to clasping their arms and legs around each other.

Almost immediately on riding into Rock Creek, Slocum heard about the train robbery. The news came in the person of T. P. Daventry who, emerging from his office onto the boardwalk as Slocum walked his horse toward the Palace de Joy, called out to him.

"Believe you're John Slocum, sir. And I'd like a word with you."

Slocum drew rein and looked down at the craggy lawman with the greying sideburns, long, bony arms, big knobby hands, and the well-worn piece of leather holstering that Navy Colt.

"Reckon you're Sheriff Daventry."

The sheriff's Stetson hat inclined slightly in assent at this statement. "Might step into my office."

Slocum liked the way the man used his words sparsely. T. P. hadn't waited for an answer, but had already turned and started back into his office.

Slocum stepped down from his horse, wrapped the reins loosely around the hitch rail, and stepped onto the boardwalk. A minute later he had seated himself in the only other chair besides the sheriff's, and had taken out a quirly and was lighting it. Meanwhile the sheriff was rolling his own.

"Heard you was in the country, Slocum," T. P. said after he'd finished his roll and had run the entire length of the cigarette along the end of his tongue, and then given an extra lick to the end before hanging it onto his lower lip. He had spoken slowly, and by the end of his sentence he'd struck his thumbnail on the wooden lucifer and regarded his visitor over the top of the flame.

"I've been trying to locate Jeremy Patches," Slocum said.

"You know something about this train holdup?" the sheriff said, ignoring Slocum's remark.

"First I've heard of it. But I did ask you about Jeremy Patches, Sheriff."

Daventry nodded. "Patches has disappeared. Might be dead. You bin out to the JP?"

"Yes."

"Then you have seen what happened."

Suddenly, the sheriff shifted in his chair so that the sunlight struck along the side of his face as it came through the dusty window. Slocum saw Daventry's eye glisten and realized it was glass. The sheriff caught his look and shifted, dropping his glance to the desk. Then he raised his eyes and looked Slocum straight in the face.

"I saw what happened," Slocum said. "But I don't know why. And there wasn't much left around the place to give any sign."

Daventry leaned back in his chair. He had taken his hat off and now crossed his arms behind his head, still holding his cigarette. "You run into anybody out there?

I'm speaking about a lawman named Myles Kincaid."

"Short fellow, mustache, small hands?"

"That is him."

"Was," Slocum said.

Daventry cut his good eye at him fast. "Dead."

"I buried him. Easy to find. He's under a pile of rocks."

"You shoot him?"

"Nope."

"Whyn't you bring him in? He was a lawman."

"I didn't know when I'd be getting into town. And I didn't know if there was any law here. I heard about the shootup."

"But you bin in town since."

"I sure have," Slocum said, thinking of the game at the Palace de Joy with High-Queen Teddy, and his marvelous bout with Ginger in bed.

"Then why didn't you report the killing?"

"I'll tell you why." And Slocum related the events leading up to and after the meeting with Mysterious Billy Dime and his companions, leaving out his encounter with Dora Patches.

"I was told you were out of town when I came in, and I wasn't here when you must have returned."

T. P. thought on that a minute. "Reckon that's right. But there's another reason you didn't talk about it. Hell, there is a council in this town. You could of told somebody."

"Not when I didn't know who those vigilantes were with or against."

Something almost like a grin, more wolfish than wry, cut into the sheriff's face for a moment. Then he said, "You're a man who knows how to take care of himself, I see."

"There isn't anybody else going to do it for me," Slocum said.

T. P. Daventry nodded. "I'll send a couple of men out for the body." He seemed to be thinking of something then, Slocum decided, as he watched the man squinting into the middle distance.

"I can see you're figurin'," Daventry said. "With a man like Mysterious Bill you never know. Well, far as the law here is concerned, the vigilantes are outside the law. Trouble is, the town favors them. Hell, they did get rid of the horse-thievin' and holdups that's been hitting this country." He leaned forward suddenly and spat hard at the spittoon next to his desk. Then, leaning back again, he resumed. "Course, I got my wonderings about some of that."

He seemed to Slocum to be speaking more to himself with those last words.

More aloud, T. P. said, "And I see you got them too." He sniffed. "Good enough." He scratched into his good eye with his thumb knuckle and then said, "You must be figurin' they're calculatin' on your leading them to Patches."

"I figure that. Nobody said it, but it's the only answer to what they did."

"You didn't see who shot that lawman, Kincaid."

"I already told you no."

Daventry grinned suddenly. "That's right, you did."

"Glad you feel you can trust me, Sheriff," Slocum said, dry as sand, and he stood up. "I'll be staying at the McCready House."

"We'll be talking."

As Slocum reached the door and put his hand on the knob, the sheriff said, "How about takin' on as deputy, Slocum? I could use a good gun."

"No thanks."

"If you change your mind let me know. It's kind of lonesome without deputies."

"Sometimes it's kind of lonesome anywhere, Sheriff."

As he went out the door and closed it behind him he wasn't sure but that he heard a cackle coming from the man in the office. But outside the day was bright and clear, and he thought he saw Ginger way down on the other side of the street, walking alone.

5

Slocum had been watching the game only a short while when it happened. It was five-handed stud and the narrow-shouldered man with the visor and the chewed-up cigar was dealing. In fact he was the house dealer, and Slocum was admiring his expertise at dealing from the bottom of the deck, or the seconds, or even from the middle.

Suddenly one of the players shoved back his chair and rose, nearly six feet of enraged sinew and muscle. His big face was purple, his eyes flaming.

"You cheap, low-down crook!" he bellowed at the dealer. "You damned cheat! That eight of clubs was on the bottom when I cut the deck. How did I get it? And how did you get that ace back of it? They should have been in the middle of the deck after the cut. You're a goddamn crook, you sonofabitch!"

"Watch your language there!" snapped the dealer, not

moving from his chair, nor taking the cigar from his mouth. He sat there with his hands in full view on top of the table and his loaded eyes on the furious man standing before him. Meanwhile, the other players had swept away from the table, only Slocum remaining seated with the dealer.

It was curious, but he had felt no danger in remaining where he was.

But the big man's hand started to move toward his hip. At that point, Slocum drew his Colt and slammed the barrel across the offended player's arm. The man let out a scream of pain and his revolver dropped to the floor.

"Why don't you two fellows just talk things over easy like," Slocum said quietly. "A misunderstanding can always be straightened out with a little patience, I am told."

The dealer remained as he was, not saying a word. The big man was trying to catch his breath, his face still twisted in pain from the gun whipping on his arm.

"You sonofabitch," he said in the next moment when he regained his breath.

The next thing anyone knew, he was flat on his back on the barroom floor where Slocum's short, chopping right fist had dumped him.

The big man wasn't finished, however; he was already pulling himself to his feet, while Slocum watched him, ready. At the same time, he was fully aware of the extraordinary calmness of the dealer, who hadn't moved an inch. And in a moment he understood why.

"That will do!" The voice was hard, cold, even as justice, and much more deadly. "This scattergun will be the next one you talk to, mister. Now get up and git out!"

Turning his head carefully, Slocum watched as High-Queen Teddy walked into the slowly spreading circle, the sawed-off shotgun easy in her hands, letting everyone understand that she knew very well indeed how to use it.

The big man was on his feet now, his breath still sawing. When he started to reach down for his gun, the voice cut into him like a whip.

"Leave it!"

Within only a moment he had left the Palace de Joy, only allowing himself the small luxury of glaring at Slocum as he went; and it was then Slocum recognized him as one of Mysterious Billy Dime's men.

"Pony," the voice said, and the little dealer moved then. "Pony, you and some others owe this gent a drink. Or two," she added. And laying the cutdown .12 gauge on top of the bar, Teddy reached up and took the cigar out of her mouth. It was unlit and looked to Slocum as though she'd been smoking it for a long time.

"Gimme a light, somebody, fer Christ sake!"

Three hands came forth with flame for Teddy's cheroot.

"Teddy, I'd like a word with you," Slocum said, "in private."

The big, gloomy head bowed into the cloud of smoke raised by the relighted cigar and a kind of gargling sound came from it. Slocum took that to mean agreement and he followed the figure toward the back of the room and through a door leaving a sign that said: NO ENTRY, AND, BY GOD, THIS MEANS YOU!

"So what can I do for you, mister?"

She had seated herself in a rocking chair, and for the first time Slocum realized that Teddy was old. There was no lack of vigor showing in that lined, leathery face, no diminution of alertness in those eagle eyes with their half-lowered lids, but it was an old person he was looking at.

"You can fill me in on what's going on in this town in respect to the vigilantes first, and then Jeremy Patches," Slocum said. "That is, if you've a mind to."

There was a knock at the office door and to the grunt that emanated from the heavily clothed High-Queen Teddy, it opened and a bartender came in with a bottle and glasses.

"You want to know about Patches and the vigilantes. Huh! Well, why not. I seen you already bin sampling the merchandise upstairs. How'd you find it, eh?" The beaming face leaned toward him, the eyes bright with humor. "Anyway, I owe you for helping out my dealer."

"Good enough," Slocum said.

"Good enough—shit! It's the best, the best this side of the Mississippi, and likely the other side too, by God! I import only the best." She belched softly into the room, removing her cigar to do so. Then she lifted her glass. "To fun!"

Slocum grinned, drinking to fun. He decided he liked the old lady, but he knew he couldn't trust her as far as he could spit.

Dutch Krone's place was a long house of the kind described as rambling, lying halfway between Rock Creek and Tilghman's Crossing. It had two floors, the ground floor being the saloon, while upstairs the girls Dutch imported from Kansas City and Denver plied their trade. It was also the favorite hangout of Mysterious Billy Dime and his vigilantes, who enjoyed relaxation between those vigorous moments when they were either breaking or enforcing the law, or both.

This particular night a meeting had been called and the members of the hardcore vigilantes were gathering to hear their leader. These numbered a dozen; at the same time, there were many more members operating on the farther reaches of the organization. These were the sort who came and went as their fortunes ran; the ranks swelling or depleting as the particular situation required. They were useful, but they were not the trusted insiders who had been there from the beginning, such as those now gathered.

At about nine o'clock a strapping man of probably thirty years named Arkansas Sullivan called the meeting to order. He banged on the bar with the heel of his big Navy Colt and announced that Mysterious Billy had arrived, and in fact was already in one of the private rooms upstairs.

The men mounted rickety stairs and filed into the gloomy room, which was lighted by a number of candles stuck into the necks of empty whiskey bottles. Maybe they were surprised, though they didn't show it, to find that Mysterious Billy was not there. They waited, most sitting on the floor, for there were only two chairs. Both, for some reason or other, were being saved for their leader.

He kept them waiting. And then in he came, striding with his big, swinging step that they all knew. Rumor had it that Mysterious Billy had spent time with an Oregon boot on his foot in prison, a contraption from which no man had ever escaped. But the story had it that Mysterious Billy was the sole exception, and had gotten out of the boot. No one knew how, and he never told. Yet, he had not only gotten out of the Oregon boot but also out of the prison.

And here he was, nodding curtly to two of the men

who were standing by the two chairs, and to nobody else. Seated on one of the chairs, he faced the gathering.

"Anyone here know how to write?"

Somebody mentioned that Burl Flanagan could handle a pen some, but then Mysterious Billy suggested Kyle Kerrigan write down a record of the meeting. This raised eyebrows but no comment. Under Mysterious Billy's direction, Kyle drew up a list of those present, and was told to keep a record of everything that happened.

"We got to keep a record of the organization," Mysterious Billy told them. "So it's legal and with the law and all like that. So we're starting now. We ain't working outside the law, we *are* the law, and we want to have papers that show that, if we ever need to show it."

"Shit, Billy, that's for a lot of them lawyer fellers," someone said from the back of the room.

"It is what we are aiming to do," their leader said. "So that's what we will do. Now, Kyle there, you start to writing." He sniffed and cleared his nose, and then said, "Mike, you help with the spellin'."

It had been the outhouse that had reminded Slocum of the hunting cabin high in the Absarokas, under Franc's Peak. The outhouse at the JP that had been destroyed totally during the fire. What he had also remembered then was the second outhouse, farther up, under the rimrocks, that he and Jeremy had built. It stood in a stand of spruce, innocent as any outhouse, but it housed a goodly supply of dynamite and other supplies that would be necessary in withstanding any sort of siege from Indian or white.

Jeremy would of course either have taken those supplies with him if he needed them, or sent Dora. For a moment he thought of riding by there to check and see if the fake outhouse was still standing, but he decided he would head directly to the hunting cabin, which would take him a day to reach if he pressed.

These thoughts didn't take long to run through him, and he was already on his way toward Franc's Peak. But now he was riding a spotted Appaloosa he'd rented from the hostler at Rock Creek, the dun having gone just a little lame, enough so that Slocum decided to rest him. He'd had his eye on a chunky little roan, but the hostler had said he was already taken, and had offered his last horse.

It was getting close to dawn when the Appaloosa settled into his stride. Slocum had spent the night at the McCready House after meeting with High-Queen Teddy, whose generous helpings of news on the tenor of the town in the face of the five killings and the train robbery with two more dead, was far more colorful than T.P. Daventry's accounts. But she offered no comment on the vigilantes. When he'd pressed her, she'd changed the subject; indeed, in such a way that he'd even liked it.

The next morning, after talking with Teddy and having had a good night's sleep, he'd had a solid breakfast at the Bean-O-Eatery. The old sourdough who ran the joint made him a rough bachelor's breakfast of beef and beans, which he washed down with Arbuckle black as tar and strong enough to build a fence.

He needed it, he soon discovered, when the livery man rented him the Appaloosa. He was a tough one, standing just under fifteen hands high, and Slocum judged about nine hundred pounds, and he looked like he could run all day. Barrel-bellied, he had thick hindquarters and shoulders and a big head with a long nose. His eyes were soft, yet bright as a chipmunk's. And Slocum was glad to have him. There'd been those few moments when the spotted horse had tried to remove him from the saddle and the sourdough's homey breakfast had almost parted company with him, but it had enough weight in it to stay down, and he'd handled that rough pony right down to a fast, steady walk out of town. As he left the corral in back of the livery he'd caught the studied look of approval on the hostler's face.

Now in the early morning dawn a slow, cold wind passed through the cottonwoods lining the Wind Water. The sky was overcast with grey clouds scudding toward the horizon, and for a moment hiding the western line of the mountains.

He rode all day into the evening, following the sun as it rode down the long sky. Now and again he stopped to rest the Appaloosa, who didn't appear to need it, being the tough little animal he was, but Slocum, like any top hand, always took first-rate care of his horse.

The sun was like a great red wafer, almost the color of blood, and shimmering as it touched the horizon. And he remembered that was a good time for an Indian attack. The warriors liked having an enemy facing into the sun at its strongest when they attacked. Instinctively he leaned his rein against the pony's neck to turn him, having already moved his eyes away from that blinding brilliance when they hit him.

Charging up out of a hidden draw which he couldn't possibly have seen, six of them came screaming at him and he was surrounded. He kept his gun holstered, seeing it was wiser not to draw, for he could tell they weren't intending to kill him, and he could only have provoked them if he'd pulled his gun.

One of them hit him across the back with his bow, almost knocking him out of his saddle. Another spat at him. But thus far that was the extent of their attack. Now they herded him away from the trail, a prisoner. Twilight had fallen by the time they reached the Indian camp.

He could feel the eyes on him as they walked their horses through the lodges which were set throughout the trees, mostly cottonwoods and box elders; yet he saw no actual person. Not far away a dog was barking.

Though he saw no one, he could feel the sullen silence in the camp. As far as he could tell they were Arapahoes, but he had no idea why they had captured him, why they had hit him, why they were angry. In any case, there was nothing he could do. And he remembered the words of an oldtimer from long ago when someone had told him the Indians and whites were at peace. "There ain't never peace with them," the old man had said. "There never will be."

At last they stopped at a tepee at the edge of the camp and one of the warriors signed for Slocum to dismount. Then two braves stripped the horse, throwing the bridle and saddle and blanket to one side. Another Indian lifted a rawhide halter over the animal's head and secured it. At that point the flap of the tepee opened and an Indian with a single feather standing up from the back of his head stepped out.

He didn't look at Slocum; his eyes were on the Appaloosa. The six who had captured Slocum were standing close to him, but he could see in their attitude that the Indian with the single feather was their chief.

The chief was still looking at the spotted horse. He

was a tall man, and he wore a large silver medal which lay flat on his broad bronze chest; a gift some of the Indian chiefs had received from the Great White Father when they visited Washington.

The eyes that had been contemplating the spotted horse now swung to the prisoner. The Indians were standing very close to him, yet no one had yet taken his weapons. The blow with the warrior's bow and the spittle evidently had been simply a venting of anger.

"This Arapaho horse," the Indian chief said. He spoke English slowly, with a kind of abrupt accent.

Slocum said, "I hired him from the livery in Rock Creek."

The chief looked puzzled and began to speak to the other Indians in Arapaho, and Slocum heard the word "hired." But he knew how to sign, which was the universal language of the plains, known by the majority of the tribes so that they could communicate.

It didn't take long for the chief to get the point. But Slocum wasn't so sure that he believed him. One of the Indians was now pointing out the brand on the pony's rump. The chief looked impassively at it.

"Steal," he said, turning again to Slocum.

"I didn't steal him," Slocum said.

An ugly murmur ran through the group then, and now more Indians appeared out of the surrounding trees and bushes. They stood there, and Slocum could feel all their eyes digging into him.

"You steal horse," the chief said, speaking into the hard silence. "You whites steal all, everywhere."

"I did not steal your horse," Slocum said evenly, staring right back at the chief.

The chief said nothing during almost a whole minute.

The Appaloosa whickered and took a step forward and pushed his muzzle against Slocum's arm.

"I Blue Cloud," the chief said.

"I'm Slocum."

"Slo—come." Blue Cloud seemed to be turning that over in his mind for a moment, and then looking hard at his prisoner he said, "You white. You know what white man do to horse stealer."

"I did not steal that horse," Slocum said.

The chief made a sign with his hand then and Slocum felt the hard poke in his back.

As he was being led away he looked up at the sky and saw the evening star.

At Dutch Krone's it was decided that an organization should be formed. That is to say, it already had been decided; by Mysterious Billy Dime. Arkansas Sullivan would be second in command; a baldheaded man named Seaborn Quince would be liaison man in Rock Creek, while Heavy Hank Perse would perform a similar function at Tilghman's Crossing.

"We need good, honest spies," Mysterious Billy said. "We got to know what's going on: when the stage shipments are being made, who struck it rich, and all like that."

Some names were mentioned for these posts, but none appeared satisfactory to Mysterious Billy.

Finally Mysterious said, "Rolfe Willing will be our man in Rock Creek. He's running the bar every night at the Palace de Joy and that's the place to hear things."

"But what about . . ." someone started to say, thinking of High-Queen Teddy and how she was sure as shooting liable to get wind of it. But he was cut off, someone shouting him down, and since he had already had plenty to drink, and was no longer as young as he used to be, he said aloud, "To hell with," and closed his eyes and fell asleep.

At the present moment, Mysterious Billy rose from his chair and sat down in the empty chair that had been standing beside him. "But we want a different set-up in Tilghman's Crossing," he said in a loud voice.

Dutch Krone said, "How about Hog Lavadure? He stinks so much nobody even seems to notice him."

The man in question didn't seem to mind this description at all for, as all eyes turned to him standing in a corner of the room in his filthy clothing, smelling of nobody was sure what, he was smiling broadly under his crust of facial filth.

"Good idea," Mysterious Billy said. "Hog, you get any information you pass it to Gillis there, and he'll pass it to me."

Hog Lavadure, who had been a wolfer until the enterprise played out in that part of the country, nodded his strange-looking head, pleased to have finally reached this level of notoriety in his long life, before he cashed in his chips.

Others were named for various jobs and responsibilities. A messenger was designated, and there were lieutenants who would plan certain types of robberies—stagecoach, railroad express cars, horses, and so on.

A few more details were dispensed with, following which the gathering removed to the floor below, there to partake of liquid refreshment.

Thus the evening ended in happy celebration, with everybody looking forward to prosperity and all the high jinks he could imagine.

It was around ten o'clock when Mysterious Billy left

the festivities, warning two trusted deputies to close down shortly so that no one would get out of hand.

"Liquor talks,' he said to Arkansas Sullivan and Seaborn Quince. You break it up if anybody starts getting too loose-like."

And with that he was gone.

Within the hour he was knocking on the front door of the brick house that stood formidably just off the road leading south out of Rock Creek, about a mile and a half from the McCready House.

"Come in," said Henry Skinner after he had ascertained that his visitor was alone. "Come into my office. We will talk."

Henry Skinner was a man whose physical appearance almost totally belied his true nature. Thin, bony, with a cadaverous face and clawlike hands, he gave the impression of a miser, a Bible-touter, a hell-and-damnation orator. He was none of these, as Ginger of the Palace de Joy could well testify. But Ginger was a person of higher intelligence than most.

Mysterious Billy was not. Yet he was good at sizing up a man as far as physical combat required. Yet, to his surprise, lately he was making little discoveries about Henry Skinner. He realized, for one thing, that Skinner hated monotony, that he had an eye for the girls, and a hand as well, and also that the man was even more ruthless than he had thought.

Thus he was only slightly surprised when Skinner suggested another train holdup. It was not something Billy would have advised, and he said so.

"They're all still hot an' bothered from the last one," he pointed out. "Not to mention the shooting in Rock Creek, with those five dead ones."

"That is precisely why we can strike," said Henry Skinner with a cold smile. He hated stupidity; and since nearly everyone was stupid, by his standards, he hated a lot of people. Dime was only one. Yet, Mysterious did have certain useful qualities. He was a true killer and he would do anything for a price. "We need to strike now simply because they won't expect it. They will be totally unaware of even the possibility of such audacity!" The eyes had thawed while he spoke and now his companion noticed the brightness and excitement coming through.

"All right then, if that's the way you want it." Mysterious Billy was nodding his head slowly, agreement on his face. Hell, he was thinking; why not? They could—or at least *he* could—likely grab a bit of the loot for himself without Skinner knowing. And it did sound like a juicy haul.

"You see," Skinner went on, "we need a distraction at this point. Something that will turn everybody's attention away from our main thrust. I am sure you understand."

"Yep." Mysterious Billy Dime nodded vigorously, his old head whipping back and forth like a hammer. "Gotcha!"

"Use your best men. And then—right away afterwards—the usual."

Mysterious Billy grinned, his teeth and gap suddenly appearing through his cracked, spittle- and tobacco-stained lips.

He saw that Henry Skinner was smiling. Suddenly a question flashed through his head as to whether old Skinner was still getting it. He had heard he visited the cribs and the girls at Teddy's. But he couldn't imagine such an old geezer making it with the girls. Hell, he had to be into seventy-some. His thoughts ran on to his own age, of which he wasn't sure, since nobody had ever kept a record, but he knew he was older than Skinner, maybe a good ten years. Close to eighty for a fact and no problem. He found his crotch heating as his thoughts turned to the new girl down at the Pastime.

But Henry Skinner was speaking. "You'll switch over quickly. First, of course, bringing the proceeds to our arranged meeting place."

"Sure. From train robbers to vigilantes. Quicker'n a hound dog with a shot of turpentine up his ass!" Mysterious Billy let out a guffaw of laughter.

In return Henry Skinner offered a wan smile. His pleasure was infinitely deeper than Dime's. For indeed, Dime knew nothing of his major plan. Therefore, the man couldn't possibly appreciate the beauty of his intricate arrangements.

It was late when his visitor left. He saw him to the door and watched him mount his horse and ride away. Late. Yet Henry Skinner was anything but tired as he locked the door of his house and walked down the hall to the guest room at the far end of the building.

"How are you, my dear?" he asked as he opened the door and then closed it behind him.

She was under the covers and his eye caught the clothes lying on the stool by the dressing table that had once been his wife's.

"How would you like it, honey?" she asked as she pushed back the bed covers and swung her feet to the floor.

"You've guessed it. Standing up. At least until my old legs give out."

"Then it'll be easy enough to lie down," Ginger said, reaching down to take hold of his rising organ.

Slocum had been taken to an empty lodge near the edge of the Arapaho village and left there. A tall warrior informed him in broken English plus signing to make sure he understood, that he must not try to escape, but that he would not be harmed. He would stay there until Blue Cloud and his headmen decided what was to be done.

He sat down on a buffalo robe, wondering if he would be given anything to eat. As though somebody had been reading his thoughts, the flap of the tent was pulled back and an Indian girl entered, bringing his hominy and jerked meat. He was hungry. At the same time, he was struck by something that told him he had seen the girl before.

She too was looking at him curiously.

"I know you—from some place," he said.

She dropped her eyes shyly, not answering.

"What is your name?"

She said nothing.

And then he remembered. "Yellow Feather?"

She raised her head and looked at him out of large, laughing brown eyes. "Slow—cum."

"At Wood River, the reservation," Slocum said.

"My people are here now," she said. "I am Yellow Feather," Her eyes went to the tent flap, then returned to him. "Eat. You hungry."

"I am glad to see you. Where is Many Horses Running?"

She didn't answer, but he thought he saw a sadness slip into her eyes.

"I . . . go."

And she was gone. He sat looking down at the food she had brought him, remembering. Remembering the Arapaho band that had been rounded up by the cavalry down at Medicine Fork and held in the meadow between Spotted Creek and the Wind Water River. He'd been scouting then for the army and had helped take the whole detachment of cavalrymen, about a dozen, plus the Indians to the reservation at Wood River. How long ago? Five, six years. He gathered now that her father, the old chief, Many Horses Running, was dead either from age or fighting. He'd been a tough old boy and Slocum had liked him. He remembered now having heard of the Arapahoes being moved from Wood River.

Well, what did that add up to? Nothing, probably. In fact, it could even work against him if they didn't remember him. He had recognized no one in the camp except the girl. Yet, Blue Cloud had repeated his name when he'd given it. Had he remembered something? Slocum didn't remember him.

He had sized up his chances of escape the moment he'd been captured, and of course again as soon as they'd put him into the lodge. It didn't look good. What was bad was the fact that they had taken him in the first place. The Arapahoes were supposedly at peace, and his capture would be a direct breaking of any agreement that the tribe had with the whites. Something must have provoked them pretty badly for them to take such an action. They were risking a lot. Yet, he saw they weren't so sure. But Slocum had certainly felt that terrible hostility when the warriors had brought him in.

Horse thieving! He could hardly believe it. All he needed now was for Mysterious Billy Dime and his vigilante gang to descend on him and wreak its particular form of "justice."

And then, something like the crack of a whip hit him. The hostler at the livery insisting on the Appaloosa being the only animal available. Was it a set-up? Had the horse really been stolen from the Arapaho camp? If so, who had stolen it, and why? He couldn't get away from the thought that Mysterious Billy Dime was somehow behind it all. But why? Why would Dime want the Arapahoes to take him? How in the hell did they expect him to locate Jeremy Patches if he was a prisoner of the Arapahoes? None of it made sense. And so he said to hell with it and lay down on the buffalo robe, closing his eyes.

They had taken his guns, his big knife, even the clasp knife he had in his pants pocket. But worst of all, he was without a horse.

Slocum did not fall asleep. He heard someone moving outside the tent, figuring it to be a guard, the rest of the camp was at rest. How to get to a horse? Or was it better to wait until the day came, when visibility and maybe even opportunity might be to his advantage?

It seemed around the middle of the night when he felt the stirring of air as the tent flap was pulled back. And immediately he smelled her.

Her touch on his face was soft as the air that had accompanied her. "Slow—come," she whispered. "I put horse by creek," And she pressed something into his hand. It was a knife.

"Yellow Feather, I wish we could be together tonight," he said. "I remember our time at Wood River."

Her lips met his and in that moment his organ stood hard as a club between his legs. The next thing he knew he was in her.

"Go," she said. "You were kind to us at Wood River. Some of us remember. I remember. You go."

But she made no move to leave him. Slowly he sank

his shaft all the way into her and let it come in great squirts. Her sigh was still warm on his face as he lifted the edge of the tepee and slid out into the starry night. Fortunately there was no moon. She had told him where the guard was, and where he could find his weapons.

Then he was down by the creek finding the horse tethered to a cottonwood. How had she managed all of it—horse as well as weapons? But she had told him that there were others who remembered him at Wood River.

Swiftly he mounted the horse—it wasn't the Appaloosa—and was on his way. He rode through the entire night and by dawn he knew that no one was following him.

It was strange, it was mysterious—the capture, the accusation of stealing the Appaloosa, then the girl and the escape. The girl and escape actually weren't so surprising. He had been helpful to the Arapahoes and to Many Horses Running that time. And he remembered too how he'd had his eye on Yellow Feather.

Well, he reflected, the old saying that all things come to him who waits has come true. And he grinned into the dawn as he thought of how it had been with Yellow Feather—in spite of themselves, despite the danger. How it had happened, and though short had been so sweet.

Some hours later he came in view of Franc's Peak, with still no sign of pursuit along his back trail.

The horse was a chunky little buckskin, just the kind of tough animal he needed. Tawny-colored except for the long black stripe running down his back from his black mane to his black tail.

It was the end of the afternoon when he crossed the thin creek and knew that he was almost at the cabin. It had taken him a while, but he had ridden extra miles to confuse any pursuit that might have been mounted. The buckskin, he decided, had been an excellent trade for the Appaloosa. Nothing like coming out best in a horse deal, he told himself.

6

It was a very warm day. The mule-drawn wagon moved slowly across the prairie, its wheels churning little puffs of dust, while the hooves of the mules kicked up small clumps of earth. It was a big wagon, and loaded fully with crates and barrels. The barrels were for various sutlers' stores, the bottles for certain high-ranking army personnel in the Territory's forts and outposts; and there was also a good supply for illegal purposes—that is, the Indians.

Two men sat on the wagon box directly behind the mules, while a third man rode an aged horse a short distance ahead.

The mules moved at their own pace. No effort on the part of any human could make them go faster. Nobody tried. The long ears of the animals bobbed with their heads at each measured step, while overhead the white sun burned down on the men, the animals, the land.

"Creek up yonder," the rider on the horse called back. "Could let 'em blow. An' us too, I reckon."

He was one of the card players who frequented the Palace de Joy. His name was Saginaw Bill Lavigne.

"Give us a rest," the driver said. Sunny Jim also frequented High-Queen Teddy's establishment. Nobody had ever known Sunny Jim to do any work other than skinning mules. He turned his head now to look at the man asleep beside him on the wagon box. "Charlie, we're about where we figgered to be. More or less," he added with a rumble in his chest which was followed by a loose, phlegmy cough.

The dozing man shook his head slightly, as though chasing a dream. He opened his eyes, squinted in pain at the heat, and quickly closed them again. He spoke slowly.

"Hotter'n a pistol in hell," he observed sagely.

The silence was fresh now as the men reached the slight shade afforded by the cottonwoods lining the banks of the creek.

Sunny Jim began sawing on the lines to bring the mules to a halt. It wasn't much of an effort; the animals were ready. After a moment Sunny Jim clucked his tongue and they stepped into the water and lowered their heads.

The men on the wagon box climbed down, and the rider dismounted. All three bent to the clear, singing stream.

Their thirst quenched, the three rose, and moved to a patch of grass by a big cottonwood. Seated, Saginaw Bill reached into his shirt to scratch vigorously at something that was biting him.

"Look at that damn fool hoss, still drinking!" And he

stood up and moved toward his horse to lead him out of the creek.

"Mules got more sense than any hoss," observed the man named Charlie. "Fool hoss'll drink hisself sick."

"Like us," Sunny Jim said. Lifting his voice, he called, "Hey Bill, bring yer bottle while you're up!"

Presently the three were enjoying themselves in the cool shade.

Suddenly Sunny Jim was serious. "Got to keep a eye out," he said. "Heard the Araps have hit the path."

"Hell, I thought we was at peace," Saginaw Bill Lavigne said, taking a stiff drink from the bottle, and passing it.

"We was," put in Charlie, whose second name was O'Moss. "But somebody bin putting out poison in the buffalo carcasses. And somebody, maybe some dog, I dunno, et it. Died, by God! Plus a white feller stole the chief's hoss. Blue Cloud, he angry!"

This brought them all into a full two minutes of helpless laughter. Gradually the great explosion of hilarity subsided and they resumed with gossip and drink.

They were all well armed with sidearms and Winchester repeaters, and they had plenty of extra ammo. These were old hands at hauling whiskey from the Union Pacific tracks near Tilghman's Crossing up to their various destinations, including the establishment of their secret employer, High-Queen Teddy.

There had been encounters with the Indians, only natural since many were customers. At the same time, there had been members of other tribes they'd encountered in a less friendly manner. But these had usually been paid off with merchandise and then had even become customers. There was thus a fairly good relationship with certain of the Shoshones, the Arapahoes, and even the Sioux.

"We'll make it to town come nightfall," Saginaw Bill predicted. "Leastways, I can. Don't know about that damn old crowbait there." He was looking at his horse.

His companions chuckled. Now they began to address themselves to some sandwiches they had brought for the occasion, some canned peaches, and not a little more of the liquor.

"What's in them heavy crates?" Sunny Jim asked suddenly.

"You mean the ones other than the whiskey?" said Charlie O'Moss.

"Shit, it don't take some schoolteacher to figger what is in them cases," Saginaw Bill said.

"What I want to know is where'n hell is Preacher? S'posed to of met up with us by now, Goddamnit!" And Sunny Jim, feeling he had been aced, spat angrily at a nearby bush.

"Preacher's s'posed to meet us at Crazy Creek, for Christ sake," snapped Charlie O'Moss. "You better lay off that there rotgut."

Muttering, Sunny Jim climbed to his feet and his companions followed suit.

"We ain't gonna make it back to town come nightfall," Sunny Jim said.

"Well," said Saginaw Bill, "what damn fool ever said we would?"

"You did, you dumb shit," Charlie O'Moss informed him.

Arguing, they left the pleasant shade by the creek and, still arguing, they continued on their way to Crazy Creek and their rendezvous with Preacher Tom.

It had been a good while since Slocum had last seen the cabin. It looked the same through the field glasses. Instead of riding directly to the log house, he had circled up onto the top of the highest rimrocks, finding the one place from where the cabin could be seen. Otherwise it might as well have been invisible; it was totally unseen until you were right in the clearing with it.

Slocum was looking for sign of life. He spotted the two horses in the corral, but only because he knew exactly where to look. And he saw a trace of smoke. No one else would have seen a thing, he knew. But still he realized that Jeremy and his daughter were being careful. It would be only chance that revealed the cabin to anyone else.

He had ridden here directly from the Indian camp, having slipped any pursuers who would surely have spotted his escape almost immediately. He hoped Yellow Feather had not been found out. And he was also hoping he would get a chance to see her again—only under different circumstances.

He waited, looking through the glasses, but nobody came out of the cabin. Obviously the girl was there, because of the sorrel horse.

It was halfway to noon when he got down to the area just above the log cabin. He had come down slowly, leading his horse, taking great care not to dislodge anything that would give him away. The buckskin was good, following his commands instantly and stepping carefully for, like any horse, he was careful of his feet.

He stopped again now at a little opening in the spruce and pine and looked at the cabin. He was almost at a level with it. Still, nobody had come outside. He moved down farther and in close to the clearing that surrounded the log structure. It was all there was, the cabin and the corral. No outbuildings save an outhouse.

He was about to move his position again, when suddenly he felt something different in the atmosphere. Putting his hand over the buckskin's nose so he wouldn't nicker if he smelled or heard another horse nearby, Slocum listened.

He waited in the silence for a long time. He was not one to question his instinct or feeling. He had felt something different, and that meant that something *was* different.

He waited, checking himself to see if he had left something undone. But he could think of nothing. He knew he had covered his trail well. He had taken great pains to do so.

And then he heard the rustle of a dry branch. He had loosened the thong on his sixgun so that he could draw quickly. Still, it could be an animal. He doubted that an Indian could have been that careless. A white? Maybe.

Slocum waited, listening, his eyes watching the cabin, his ears aware of his immediate surroundings. And then two things happened.

The cabin door opened and Dora came out. And he felt the wind touch his face and he smelled bear grease.

He felt the whoosh of wind as the stone hatchet flew within inches of his head. Something had told him to duck, and that "something" saved his life. In the next moment he had grabbed the big buck by his hair as he charged, had fallen rolling onto his back, at the same time kicking the Indian hard in the crotch and throwing him far over his head. In a flash Slocum was back up on his feet, noting that his attacker was a Shoshone. The Indian rose slowly, his face twisted in pain. But Slocum knew a lot of it was faking. In the next split second the Indian had drawn a knife and charged.

Slocum shifted his stance, half turned away, then turned back and kicked the Shoshone as hard as he could in his kneecap. The Indian released a huge grunt and staggered. Slocum slammed him in the stomach, doubling him, then brought his big fist down hard behind the man's ear in a rabbit punch, killing him instantly.

"Get into the cabin," he said to the girl. "There could be others with him."

He took a close look at his attacker to make sure he was dead, then waving to the girl to get back into the cabin, he slipped into the trees and backtracked the Shoshone's trail till he found his horse. There was no sign of any other pursuers.

"He must've taken off on his own to find me," he told Dora when he reached the cabin. "At least that's what I hope; that he's alone. Course, he could have been sent."

"And I hope he was alone," said Jeremy Patches, coming to the door behind his daughter.

"Boy, you are a good one to see at this point," said Slocum, laughing. "I'd about given up on you."

"And me on you, John." Patches, a man of about fifty, was still trim, but he was limping. There was a broad smile of welcome on his face.

"Bullet hurt some," he went on, "but it went all the way through, so I'm on the mend." His smile turned to a laugh as he saw Slocum looking at his leg. "I know, you don't believe me, just like Dora."

He was a tall man, though not quite as tall as Slocum. His forehead was wide and he had light grey eyes.

Like his daughter's eyes, they were bright and clear and Slocum knew, often full of fun.

"By God, John, it's good to see you, you son of a gun!" He nodded toward the window. "I'll give you a hand. We'd better get him away from the front there, just in case we have any more visitors."

"I want to look him over more closely," Slocum said. "He's not from Blue Cloud's people." And he quickly told the two of them about his adventure with the Arapahoes.

Together the two men examined the dead Indian carefully. "He is one big bugger," Jeremy said. "I watched you from the window there. Had the Winchester trained right on him if things had got too hot." He gave a grim chuckle. "Knew you'd handle him."

"He's Shoshone, I'm pretty sure," Slocum said. "What puzzles me is what he was doing here. I would have expected the Arapahoes cutting my trail."

Jeremy looked at the sky, then down at the ground. He cocked his head at Slocum. "What d'you figure?"

"I am figuring he was looking for you or me, or both."

"You mean, independent of Blue Cloud's band?" Dora asked. She had been standing silently watching and listening to the two men.

"Right. I also understand there've been some renegades around, hitting some of the ranchers and travelers," Slocum said. "Except I don't think he was one of those," He paused, then said, "No, I reckon somebody was covering his bets."

"You're saying he was hired," Jeremy said.

Slocum nodded.

"But why?" Dora asked. "Why would he be following you, John?"

"Because somebody wants to keep an eye on me, hoping I'll lead them to you and your father." And then he added, "But I've got a notion he didn't follow me here. I checked my back trail close. I think he got here by himself, maybe even by accident."

Slocum had turned away from them and walked toward the trees. "I'll strip the buckskin," he said. "And if you've got feed?"

"Sure have." Dora stepped forward. "You'll be stopping?"

"You bet. Only for a spell. I'll be pulling out come morning."

She had been leading the way to the corral and now she stopped and turned to face him. "So soon?"

He could see the disappointment in her face.

"Whatcha going to do, John?" Jeremy asked before Slocum could answer the girl.

"Comes daylight I'll be backtrailing that feller so's we don't have whoever it is who's so curious about you and me dropping in here."

In the cool pre-dawn he saddled the buckskin and started out from the cabin. His plan was to backtrail the Shoshone to find out if he had come from some renegade band, or had perhaps been hired independently by a white, possibly Mysterious Billy Dime.

Light was coming into the sky quickly now, and he rode with care, staying under cover of the trees as much as possible, and never riding along the horizon. He smelled rain.

It had been good meeting up with Jeremy again. Good to verify that his old friend was still alive. They had stayed up late after supper talking over the situation with the JP and the cattlemen. Dora had stayed with the two men while they nursed their drinks and smoked in the one-room cabin.

"First I thought it was the cattlemen," Jeremy explained, "the big stockgrowers like Link Watson and Chuck Donohue and them others that wanted the place. See, it's a lot shorter route to get the cattle up onto the mountain in summer if you just go right smack dab through my place."

"Excepting it wasn't that?" Slocum said, his tone questioning as he studied his friend.

"It wasn't that. Hell, that was too damn obvious, and besides, I'd let 'em have some kind of right of way if they wanted to approach me in a decent way."

"I know what you mean," Slocum said ruefully. "Those stockmen think they're all angels of the Lord."

"Anyway," Jeremy continued after taking a long pull at his drink, "anyway, it became clear that there was something bigger going on than cattle."

Slocum's eyebrows lifted. "Like what? Would you be meaning, like somebody stirring up the tribes?"

"I always said you were quick, John."

"Only way for a man to keep his scalp."

They all three had a laugh at that.

"But I do notice the Arapahoes are raspy," Slocum said. "And I have heard rumors of maybe the Indian Agent being changed. Graft going on; all of the usual, but more so. It's something I been smelling since I rode into these parts."

"You smelled right," Jeremy said, nodding and leaning forward in his chair, his drink in one hand, his cigar in the other. "There is something brewing."

"Has it got anything to do with Mysterious Billy Dime?" Slocum had asked.

"I do believe it has got to. That gentleman has

changed things right around in Rock Creek and environs," Jeremy said. He looked over at his daughter, who had been listening and not saying much during the conversation. "That right, Dora? Would you say it was like that?"

"I would. It is surely like that. It's been getting worse since the killings of the five people in town. I don't know who those men were, but I know Rock Creek isn't the same since that terrible night. I don't know if it ever will be."

"Daventry thinks the train holdup at Medicine Gap was maybe the same bunch."

"I wouldn't be surprised," Slocum had said. "I wouldn't be surprised if somebody is trying to put the wind up Rock Creek and maybe a few other places."

"Trying to show everybody they need the vigilantes, is what you're saying."

Slocum had nodded. "Maybe."

They had chewed it a good while and then it was late. He had watched the girl getting sleepier, and finally the sound of heavy breathing coming from his host had brought an end to the evening of pleasant reunion, reminiscence, and conjecture.

She had shown him where to sleep, in the far corner of the cabin. They were all together in the one room, and as she stood in front of him saying good night he could feel his own warmth and hers mingling. Her eyes were shining and he told her that they looked like clouds.

She had said nothing, but he felt something move from her toward him. In the early morning she was ready with coffee for him.

Now, following the Shoshone's back trail, he felt a great relief to know they were both there, back at the cabin, alive and together. He would surely do his best to keep it that way. Funny, he was suddenly thinking, how Jeremy had got it in his leg. Like himself when the big sorrel stud horse had fallen on him. It was Jeremy who had rushed in, sacking the excited animal away from him, or he would surely have been tromped. And it had been Slocum's leg that time.

In a little while it began to rain, wiping out the Shoshone's trail, which had been hardly visible anyway. He turned the buckskin toward Rock Creek. He had decided he wanted to see T.P. Daventry. There were some things he needed to know about the Indian Agent and the Arapaho reservation agreements, and he hoped the sheriff would be able to tell him what he wanted.

Shortly after ten o'clock at night the stationmaster at Big Spring heard sounds that brought him to the window of his tiny shack. He shook his head.

"Hearin' things, must be. Could of swore I heard horses."

"Wouldn't be surprised," his assistant said indifferently. "Could be passengers for the ten o'clock."

The "passengers" appeared shortly in the persons of Arkansas Sullivan, Kyle Kerrigan, Heavy Hank Perse, and some others, including Mysterious Billy Dime. All were heavily masked as they marched into the station.

The stationmaster and his assistant raised their hands without waiting for any order.

"Tie 'em," said Mysterious Billy, his voice muffled by his thick mask.

Just as the last knot was being tied, a train whistle moaned in the distance. As the bandits scattered to strategic positions, the train, trailing sparks from the locomotive stack, pulled to a stop.

With almost the precision of military drill, Mysterious Billy and his men mounted their attack. Not as much as a minute passed from the time the engineer and his fireman were ordered to throw up their hands till the moment when Mysterious Billy and Arkansas Sullivan climbed into the express car.

"Get that safe open right now!" Mysterious Billy ordered. The messenger's jaw dropped open.

"Can't, mister. It's a time lock. Can't be opened till we get to Cheyenne."

"That's a lie!" snapped Arkansas Sullivan. Jumping forward, he shoved the barrel of his gun right into the messenger's big belly. "You open that safe there right now or your guts'll be all over this car!"

"He ain't lyin'," Mysterious Billy said. He had been studying the safe. "Nobody can open the goddamn thing. But looky yonder!"

In a small, heavily built box were a number of oblong packages. Mysterious Billy lifted one of these, cursing happily at the weight, and smashed the package against the corner of the box. A shower of twenty-dollar gold pieces spilled to the floor.

"This here is what we want!" Billy cried with delight. "By God, this here's a minted gold mine!"

Fifteen or twenty minutes later, after the coaches had been raided and the passengers robbed, the gang withdrew. For effect, a few shots were fired as the bandits raced for their horses and pounded away into the covering night.

Within twenty-four hours the money had been deposited in a secret place given by Skinner to Mysterious Billy Dime — later to be divided "according to worth." Following a short rest of men and horses, the very same personnel, with some additions, were in hot pursuit of the "villains" who had robbed the train at Big Spring.

As Seaborn Quince observed to the stationmaster and his assistant at Big Spring, "Woe to them jaspers who thinks they can escape the justice of the vigilantes."

"What about the sheriff?" said the stationmaster sourly. "Ain't he the law in Rock Creek and this here country?"

Seaborn Quince spat indolently at a small bug moving across the stationhouse floor. "The sheriff is one man."

"Then them vigilantes could be helpin' him is how I sees it," said the stationmaster. But he didn't like the look that came into Seaborn Quince's eyes at that moment. And it made him wonder.

In the back room at the Palace de Joy, High-Queen Teddy sat alone at the round baize-top table. She was playing solitaire, a favorite pastime, especially when she was trying to think something through.

As usual, Teddy was dressed warmly, with her customary collection of shawls, scarves, sleeves, collars, belts, bandannas, and sometimes, though not now, even gloves. Her cold, unlighted cigar was clamped firmly in her teeth. Occasionally she removed it in order to let fly at the spittoon which was within easy range, but she invariably missed.

Now, as a thought struck her, she was moved sufficiently to strike a wooden match and relight the black stub. In a moment her head, covered with a bandanna underneath an antique felt hat, was enveloped in smoke.

There was a knock at the door and a voice called, "Teddy, you busy in there?"

"Come, for Christ's sake!" The words came harshly

around the fat stogie, falling upon the baldheaded bartender, Skinhead Miller, as he entered, wiping his hands nervously on his filthy apron.

"Why do you ask such a dumb question like was I busy? Hell, ain't I *always* busy? You ever see me when I *wasn't* busy? You think this place could get run without me being busy, huh? Night and day? Busy!"

She had continued to play as she delivered this speech, which Skinhead and everyone else knew backward and forward, her eyes remaining on her cards, not once looking up at the bartender, her head wreathed in smoke.

"Mr. Skinner sent a message,"

The leathery lids of the eyes flicked open, and their owner regarded this information frigidly.

"What's it say?"

"Says he will be coming by for some refreshment later tonight and hopes to see you for a game of cards."

"Who told it, the message?"

"Burleigh Harrigan."

A silence fell, and presently Skinhead thought he heard something, and at the same time he was aware of the scent of onion. Then he realized that he was hearing a kind of whistling of a popular tune, barely recognizable, which was issuing from his employer's cracked lips as she continued her game of solitaire. The odor of onion was coming from the same source.

"What'll I tell him, Teddy?"

"Who?"

"Burleigh."

"Tell him nothin'." Her eyes didn't move from her cards as she continued her play.

"But he's waitin'; I mean, Skinner expects an answer."

Instantly the head shot up, the eyes bulleting the barkeep, who realized his error too late.

"I don't give a shit who's waitin' for what. Now get the fuck outta here. This here's my place, and I'll be here or I won't be here, whenever I feel like it, doin' my business or havin' fun. You tell that son of a bitch out there to tell Skinner if he wants to talk to me he can get his ass over here and see if—I am saying *if*—I am—" She broke off in mid-sentence, apparently at a loss for words. But no—all at once her face screwed up into a haughty display of perhaps her idea of a countess as the gargling voice now trilled out its vulgar rendition of high society speaking to a member of the lower class. "I am saying *if* I happen to be *receiving . . . !*"

Skinhead Miller's eyes bugged out at this sudden appearance of one of Teddy's many roles. He was even more shaken when he heard the cackling that seemed to start somewhere in his employer's bosom and came roaring out of her wide, wet mouth.

"Now haul ass, my lad! There! By Jesus, there's that goddamn queen I bin lookin' for!" And she slammed the red queen down onto the place where it decided the game in her favor.

"And bring me another drink!" she roared after the departing bartender.

In the next moment, the room was filled with silence as she collected the cards, quickly fitted them into a deck, and then broke the silence with the riffle and shuffle as only an expert can do it.

It had to happen. Slocum had all along known it had to happen. And of course at the most inconvenient moment! Just as he drove deeper into her—up high, and really hitting the end of her as they came together in a rush of impossible ecstasy, every inch of their bodies thrashing to a climax, the ancient bed crashed to the floor, its springs undone, the whole room shaking under the impact of bed and thrusting bodies. Nor did those bodies even hesitate in their mad delight, but kept stroking into the ultimate joy of their union.

"Jesus!" the girl managed to say at last.

"That was the shot heard 'round the world," Slocum whispered into her ear.

From below they heard a roar and loud cursing coming up violently through the cracks in the old floorboards.

"What's below us?" Slocum asked.

"I'll give you one guess," she said, disentangling her legs and arms.

"High-Queen Teddy's office."

"I just hope she doesn't take a notion to come busting up here."

But his reply was interrupted by a stick banging on the ceiling of the room below, and now they could hear Teddy's bellowing tones.

"You fuckers think this here place is a whorehouse or somethin', for Christ's sake! Shut up, up there!"

"Sorry, Teddy," Slocum called down. "Thought we were in church."

Ginger had whipped her hands up to his lips, but she was too late to stop him. At the same time, she could hardly control her laughter.

And then they realized he had said the right thing. A strange rumbling sound was heard in the room below, mixed with a heavy, gasping breathing.

"She's laughing," Ginger said. "The old bitch has got a lot of fun in her. No fooling."

"You've got a lot of fun in you, young lady," he said.

"And you've got a lot of ding-dong, young fellow."

He had rolled off her, but remained close, with his leg thrown over her and his arm under her head.

"Somebody told me you kept company with Mr. Henry Skinner," Slocum said suddenly. "That so?"

"What? You jealous?"

"No, I'm not. But I need to know something like that. I need to know if I can trust you."

"You can trust me," she said. "Just remember I'm a poor working girl."

"I promise not to forget it."

After a moment she said, "Do you trust me?"

"I don't trust anybody." And then he added, "I like you."

She turned toward him then, and the calf of his leg slipped around her buttocks.

"I'll settle for that, Mr. Slocum."

He could feel her wetness on his rising organ. "Will you settle for this?"

Reaching down to guide him inside her she said, "Any time. Any place. Just as often as you want it."

In her room directly beneath Ginger's, High-Queen Teddy gazed insolently upon Henry Skinner, who was sweating a great deal.

"Jesus Christ, Skinner, when the hell you gonna grow up?" The words came out sharp, the eyes turning into malevolence as she observed Skinner's discomfiture. "You jealous of a little whore like that? Come on!"

"Of course not. Of course I'm not jealous! Why would I be jealous? What's the matter with you?"

He had taken out a large white handkerchief and was mopping his shiny brow. Now he wiped around his collar.

Suddenly the atmosphere in the room changed. Skinner felt suddenly clammy with a kind of fear. The voice that now came across the baize-top table was nothing at all like the High-Queen Teddy he had known until a minute ago. The voice purred, the words slipping out on little tracks of honey. Those lizard eyelids blinked up and down. And Henry Skinner thought he was going to be sick.

"You could do worse, Henry, my lad. I've had the experience, and that's what counts. I used to keep going at it all night. I'd wear out half a dozen of them cow pushers in one night. And I ain't lost my skill. You can do better'n that piece upstairs. You want a woman your age, a woman with your experience, my lad! Not some half-assed little whore like that one!" And she jerked her thick thumb toward the ceiling.

"I don't know what you're talking about!" Skinner had regained enough control of himself to sound stern.

"Come off it! You know damn well what I mean. And I wouldn't even be surprised if you sicced her onto Slocum."

"For heaven's sake, Teddy, why would I do such a thing?"

"To get information, you asshole. Bed's a hundred times better than the confession box, believe you me. And I know, while you may be dumb about women, you sure ain't stupid when it comes to money and your own interests."

Her words pierced him, while her relentless eyes and vulgar tone made him want to vomit. "I mind my own business, Teddy, if that's what you mean," he said, trying to draw on his ruptured dignity.

"Bullshit! I know you been humping that damn Ginger. I'll bet you're paying her extra, 'cause she doesn't kick back much to yours truly, her benefactor! By God, I lifted her out of the gutter, I did!"

Teddy's return to her former vulgarity and aggression had been as abrupt as her switch to peaches and cream, and now she was back again. Her eyes swept up and down his chest, lingering on his mouth, then moving slowly over his cringing face.

"Henry, think it over. You could do worse. A whole lot worse. I could give you a real good time. It wouldn't cost you a cent, neither." And she slapped her fingers down onto the top of the table, as though closing the deal.

Skinner felt his whole insides drop to his feet. Somehow he managed to stand up.

"I want you to talk to that man Lavigne and his helpers. We'll increase the whiskey to the tribes. I want them to get plenty."

His plan worked. Teddy switched immediately back to business. "You want the whole country to get shot up by them redskins?" she demanded. "I know you bin sending in guns, too."

"Only some. Only one crate."

"You mean one crate—this time."

"I want them to put pressure where it's going to hurt."

"You want them chased or moved—whatever—off their reservation, is what you mean," High-Queen Teddy said, her loaded eyes pinning him to the door he was now standing against.

"I mean just what I say!" He had regained himself now and his tone was as hard as hers. The personal interlude which she had created—probably as a gambit, he told himself—had horrified him, for not in any imaginable way was he able even to consider her talk seriously. His flesh crawled as his thought touched just the bare edge of their recent conversation.

High-Queen Teddy knew where her bread was buttered, and she resumed the role in which he knew her best, the only one he could accept.

"I'll talk to them," she said, picking up the deck of cards. She gave the deck a quick shuffle and placed it carefully on the table right in front of her.

"Cut you for high card, Skinner, my boy."

"Another time." He started to open the door.

"Come on, Skin! Just one fast cut. I win it, then you got to do it to me. If you win, then I got to do it to you!"

Her roaring cackle followed him out of the room as he almost ran to get away. He could still hear her booming laughter through the closed door, and the big grin on the baldheaded bartender's face didn't help his humor at all.

7

The country beyond Tilghman's Crossing was lonely on the night end of the run from Cedar Butte. The road was a lot like a switchback over the hard terrain and the Concord swayed uneasily behind the six coach horses. D. D. Bones, holding the ribbons, threw an anxious glance over at the massive shadows falling down from the rise of mountain to the west. There was a fair moon, but too many shadows, he was thinking, as he slipped a glance over to the dark hills on the east. And too many dry washes and rocks to make him feel easy. Nor was he happy about the thick brush crowding the road.

D. D. Bones tried to keep his thoughts off the five thousand dollars in coin and paper in the treasure box and the young greener riding shotgun on the seat next to him. D. D. would have preferred any of the older men who had more experience and very likely sounder judgment in a tight than young Tom whatever-his-name-was.

The messenger obviously didn't feel any of the trepidation of D. D. beside him. He sounded thoroughly bored, in fact, as his voice cut into D.D.'s gloomy thoughts.

"Where are we?"

"Deal Creek's just yonder," D.D. Bones said, and as he spoke he drew a heavy gold watch from his vest pocket and checked the time with his schedule. In the meager light he could just make out that it was around eleven and he was pretty close to being on time. He had just put the watch, a gift from his father-in-law, back into his pocket when he heard the shout and his heart sank.

"Pull up, driver! And don't make any trouble! You are well covered!"

Tom, the messenger, bristled beside him, and D.D. thought, the kid's full of piss and vinegar, the damn fool; so he nudged him with his elbow as he pulled on the lines to halt the horses.

There were two men, masked, holding rifles, and one of them moved immediately toward the lead horse nearest him. D.D. had no notion at all of trying to make a run for it. There was no need for him to point out to his young companion that half a dozen men had suddenly appeared from behind rocks at the side of the road. The green lad saw them clearly and he made no move toward the shotgun lying on his lap.

The larger highwayman walked right up to the driver's box now. D.D. set the brake, making sure the man below saw just what he was doing, and then he put his hands in the air. He knew the nervous ones sometimes shot up a whole load of passengers, and he wasn't taking any chances on a fast move of hand or foot being misunderstood.

"Throw down the shotgun," the bandit said to the messenger.

He caught the piece one-handed, stepped back and smashed it over a nearby rock, then tossed what was left of the gun into the night.

"Now throw down the chest."

"Can't do it, mister," D.D. said. "It's chained on."

"Both of you get down, then."

The two stagemen dropped down carefully from the box. It was a familiar scene to D. D. Bones—he'd been held up twice before—but it was the greener's first. The two stagemen were lined up with the passengers, their backs to the man with the gun who was giving the orders. Now the smaller of the two bandits came back to where they were all standing and covered them while the big man mounted the box. Using a big stone he'd picked up from the side of the road, he broke the chain that secured the box to the boot. It was easy enough to remove what was inside.

Then the big man ordered everyone to empty their pockets and put their contents into the sack his companion held out as he passed before them.

Then everyone was ordered back onto the stage and the driver was told to get going.

Leaving the Palace de Joy in such haste as he had, Henry Skinner skidded on some loose slop that was just outside the batwing doors on the boardwalk and twisted his ankle. The result was that he was now reduced— physically at any rate, though not mentally or emotionally—to using a cane. And he found the cane could also have another use, as he was now showing Mysterious Billy Dime, waving it angrily at that old man. Dime took a step backward, though not in fear so much as in the realization that Skinner might strike him by accident.

"You old fool!" Skinner snarled. "You come and tell me about this great stage holdup, but what about Slocum! Eh? What about Slocum!"

"But shit, Henry, we done hauled in five—I says *five thousand* dollars!" He grinned, his old face wreathed in superior knowledge as though mollifying a child. "Think of all them fine Havana cigars you can buy in San Francisco!"

"And what happened to that Indian tracker, scout or whatever he was? He has disappeared; that's what's happened to him! And that was your idea. You know what that double-crossing redskin found out about Slocum and Patches? Not one damn thing! And the son of a bitch has cut out. Vanished!"

"Could be Slocum come upon him and . . ." He drew his long forefinger across his wrinkled throat. "Could be."

"Well then, now what? I want Patches; and I mean now!"

"I told you I'd find Patches. And so Slocum pulled something, but I got a notion where to look."

"Where?" Henry Skinner's jaws were working fast, as though he was trying to find something to spit out. "Listen, Dime, I hired you for certain jobs. One of those jobs was to keep close to Slocum, so he would lead us to Patches. Once we get Patches we can bust any of those small ranchers we want."

"Thought you just wanted Patches's spread."

"His is the main one. But they all need to know who is going to be running things around here." He paused, took out a cigar, and lighted it. "Now, matter of fact, you did well with the stage. That gives four big robberies. Now, do what you are able, and I mean do it! Round up some men for a hanging party. Round up those men who shot up Rock Creek, and also robbed the two U.P. trains. And you must get them before the Union Pacific sends men down here. Mind Daventry, by God. I don't want him getting too riled up. And you tie those two train robberies in with the stage and the thing in town here. Now, then, in that sweep you can pull in Slocum."

"But what if he hasn't led us to Patches yet?"

"You will beat it out of him. Starve him. Anything, don't kill him until you get that information." In the excitement of talking he had started to wave his hand, in which he was holding his fresh cigar. Suddenly the long, thin panatella flew out of his fingers and hit Mysterious Billy Dime right in the chest.

At once a charged silence hit the room, which happened to be Skinner's office at the McCready House in Rock Creek. The two men stood hard as rock staring at each other, neither giving an inch of ground.

Henry Skinner felt a sudden surge of happiness in his bony body, something he hadn't experienced in some time. The grisly scene with the unexpectedly amorous High-Queen Teddy had unsettled him almost totally— no wonder he'd injured his ankle!—but now, under the lash of necessity, he was master of himself again. Ah, it was good. And he gloated at the other man's indecision. Clearly, Mysterious Billy Dime was torn between rage and prudence. Money, and the knowledge that Skinner had of his operations prior to their association, tempered him. Skinner watched the fight going on in the old man, and he exulted.

Slowly, Henry Skinner withdrew a fresh cigar from the pocket of his frock coat, bit off the end, turned his head slightly to spit out the bullet, and then lighted up.

As he blew out his first cloud of smoke, the ultimate test sprang right into his thought. He almost smiled as he said. "Care for a cigar, Dime?" And his eyes dropped to the cigar on the floor, then rose to look right into the eyes of Mysterious Billy.

"I'll take one of those," Mysterious said, nodding toward Skinner's breast pocket where the tops of two cigars showed.

"Of course—of course!" Henry Skinner reached up with one hand and took out a cigar and handed it to Dime, while with his other hand he moved his cane to flip away the cigar that was lying between them on the floor.

He could see to his pleasure that this theatrical game was not lost upon his companion. But now, counter-sinking the nail was even better.

"I have another appointment now, Dime. And, by the way, if you really want to know where John Slocum might be, you might try the verandah over the barroom at Teddy's Place. At least, that is where he was last night. I wouldn't be surprised if he were still there, or at any rate in town—here, in Rock Creek!" And he laid into those last words. "You will excuse me now."

Slocum heard the news of the two latest holdups from T. P. Daventry, but not in the way he might have expected. He had been unable to locate the sheriff when he'd rid-den into town the evening before, and was surprised when the knock came on his bedroom door, followed by the sheriff's voice.

"Slocum, it's Sheriff Daventry. I'd like a word with you."

Slocum had already drawn his gun and was standing

beside the door, ready for whatever action followed.

"Are you alone?"

"I am alone."

It was early morning, but Slocum was already up, and had been lying on his bed thinking over the situation he was finding himself in so suddenly. He was also feeling a strong urge to get back to the cabin with Jeremy and Dora Patches.

When he let the sheriff in he stepped aside, still holding his gun in case anyone suddenly followed.

"You don't trust me?" Daventry said laconically with a wry grin as Slocum closed and locked the door behind him.

"I don't trust anybody," Slocum said.

T.P. nodded in agreement with that statement.

"What can I do for you, Sheriff?"

Daventry told him about the Big Spring train robbery and the holdup of the Tilghman–Rock Creek stage.

"You say they already knew what was aboard the stage?" Slocum said, sitting on the edge of his bed.

The sheriff nodded, tipped his hatbrim up with his forefinger, and sniffed. He was sitting in the one chair with its back facing Slocum, leaning his arms across the wood frame. "They went right to it."

"So what do you want with me? You thinking I had a hand there?"

"I want you to help me."

"I told you I don't want to take on as a deputy."

"I am figuring you want to help Jeremy Patches and his daughter."

"I see you get around, Sheriff."

"That is what I'm paid for."

"I want to know why Dime and his vigilantes are putting pressure onto Jeremy," Slocum said. "They've got to be the ones who fired his outfit. I want to know are they working alone, or with somebody, and maybe for somebody else. What can you tell me?"

"All I know is they're not unpopular in town, in Rock Creek," Daventry said. "Everybody says they cleaned out the horse thieving and the road agents. Only now we have got three new robberies and killings." He paused and, taking out a wooden match and quickly whittling a point with his clasp knife, he began picking his teeth. "That's besides the town getting shot up when we lost the last sheriff," he added.

Slocum realized he was hungry and hadn't eaten in some time.

The sheriff said, "Sure, they caught up with some suspects, and they claim they're gonna bring justice and this time turn 'em over to the law. But I ain't seen hide nor hair of one of 'em." He stopped picking at his teeth and let the wooden pick stay in his mouth as he said, "Reckon you know how I am figurin' it; that is, am still figurin' it"

Slocum nodded. "It's an old story, ain't it? But how can you get the proof on it? Way I see it, the town wants the vigilantes, and of course, they'll play it both ways. I am thinking something else though," he went on, leaning forward. "I'm thinking those killings and robberies, all close together, could be a way to draw anyone off from something else. In fact, the whole vigilante thing might be just that."

T.P. raised his eyebrows at that, and his lower lip jutted forward. "Huh, he said. "Huh . . ."

"I am thinking of the whiskey, and a crate of guns I seen sign of, and how the Arapahoes are getting kind of feisty."

"How so?"

Slocum told him about his adventure with the Appaloosa and Blue Cloud.

"They're riled about something. That's easy to see."

"I know that," Daventry said. "They don't like where they are; meaning they don't really like any kind of reservation. I personally don't see where they are is so bad. They got good water, feed, and game."

"They don't like being prisoners," Slocum said. "No matter how fancy you paint the walls."

T. P. Daventry looked at Slocum closely. He'd heard Slocum was part Cherokee.

Slocum felt his appraisal, knew what was going through his mind. "That's not the point," he said. "There's something else. Somebody is getting them whiskey and guns. I'm beginning to think somebody wants them off the reservation."

He held up his hand as Daventry started to speak. "I know we spoke about that already. What I'm saying is the Arapahoes, they're not really wanting the whiskey and guns. I know something about Blue Cloud, and some years back I knew the old chief, Many Horses Running. They're peaceful; they want peace. Sure, there are some young ones who get ratchety and hit the path now and again, but the tribe isn't like that. My notion is somebody's deliberately trying to rile them."

"Question is why." The sheriff laced his fingers together on the back of the chair and leaned his chin on his hands. His glass eye stared blankly at Slocum. Then he canted his head and looked at him with his good eye.

"Question is also what this could have to do with Jeremy Patches," Slocum said. "I am thinking land."

"There ain't nothing on that land of the Araps excepting like I said—grass, game, and water."

"And there isn't anything on Jeremy's land but the weather," Slocum said drily.

"I ain't heard of any strike anywhere," T.P. said.

"What about right-of-way? Any rumor about a railroad going through?"

"Where the hell would it go to?"

"Jeremy and Dora Patches both told me they'd thought of the stockgrowers wanting a short route to get their beeves up onto the mountain comes summer, but Jeremy said he would have worked something out with them."

"And far as I know, nobody's been nosing around to buy up land anywhere near them two places," Daventry said. "The sections butting up to Patches's JP ain't worth the shovel you'd buy to try digging. Most of it dry as a bone and just as hard."

"Well," Slocum said after releasing a long sigh and reaching to his pocket for a smoke, "well, it does look like somebody's throwing up a lot of smoke to cover something. About the Arapaho end of the stick, I don't have a notion. But it is clear somebody is after Jeremy's place."

"I'll cover that," T.P. said and he began building himself a smoke, while Slocum struck a match on his trouser leg and lighted a quirly.

"You gonna help me?" the sheriff said, canting his head so his good eye could take in Slocum.

Slocum stood up, lifted his hat, and ran his big hand over his thick black hair, then put his hat back on his head. "What the hell do you think I been doing all this time, Sheriff, just standing here pickin' my nose?"

• • •

The more he thought about the situation, the more Slocum realized Jeremy and Dora Patches didn't have much time left. The situation was getting worse fast. What was more, Slocum wasn't at all fooled by Jeremy saying that his leg was about good as new. He had seen the grimacing, the draining of color from his friend's face when he was limping and thought no one was noticing. He knew Dora was well aware of her father's condition, but evidently Jeremy had sworn her to keep quiet.

All this was going through his mind as he reached the top of the stairs in the McCready House and started down the corridor to his room. It was late and he'd just left the Palace de Joy where he'd sat in on a game of stud and about broken even. What was bothering him was how to work out a plan of action, yet he didn't want to force anything either.

He had just started his key into the doorlock when the door behind him and across the narrow corridor opened and two men came out. At the same instant his own door was yanked open from the inside and the next thing he knew something like a pistol barrel had been laid right alongside his jaw.

As he went down in a red haze of pain, he could feel the boots, the fists, the elbows and knees. They had him on the floor of his room. The wind had been knocked out of him. His back felt as though it was broken, and his head was screaming.

Opening his eyes to slits, he found the kerosene light being held right to his face. He was choking with something—blood or spittle, he didn't know what.

"Slocum, you son of a bitch—where is Patches?"

It was Dime leaning down, breathing his rat breath into Slocum's torn face.

"Tell me where Patches is!"

"Dunno." The word might have sounded, he wasn't sure. Maybe it had only been in his mind.

"Yes you do. An' you're gonna tell me! Slocum!"

He must have passed out, for the next thing he knew he felt water in his face, going down his throat and up his nose, and he was gagging and fighting for air.

"Where's Patches?"

"He's dead, you son of a bitch!"

"You're lying."

He said nothing. Maybe he passed out again. Afterwards, trying to reconstruct the scene, he couldn't remember; he didn't know what happened until he felt himself pulled to his feet. Something hit him in the face. A wet towel, rolled into a tight tail and cutting like bullwhip into his face.

He was on his back on the floor, having kicked somebody in the crotch. Someone was kneeling right into his neck. He could barely breathe.

Again Dime's foul breath was in his face. "Slocum, this is a warning. The last warning. You leave here in the morning, we're going to follow you to Patches. Because that is where you're going. You hear me!"

"I hear you."

"You're going to lead us to where Patches is hiding. You do that or you will die. I mean slowly. Slocum, you ever see a man staked out by the Injuns on a anthill in the noontime?"

"Dunno where Patches is. Told you . . . dead. He dead." He could hardly get the words out, and again he wasn't sure whether he was actually speaking or just thinking the words.

He must have said them aloud, because the next thing he knew was a tremendous blow in the ribs, another on the biceps of his gun arm.

"That'll take care of any gunplay for a spell," somebody snarled.

Again he must have passed out. When he started to come around there was daylight at the windowsill. It had taken him a while to come to himself, for he kept slipping back into the dark. Finally, desperation won and he pulled himself to his knees, using the bed for support. Then, after much effort, he stood. He had to hold onto the bedstead to keep from falling. But they hadn't taken his extra gun, which he had hidden under his mattress.

He knew he looked a mess, but he did nothing to clean himself up. And as he went downstairs he almost tripped and fell, even staggered a little on purpose. Out of his swollen left eye he noticed the room clerk watching him, with fear all over his face.

For several moments he stood on the verandah breathing in the smell of the town, horses, the prairie, and his own sweat. Then he walked down to Oren's Eatery and ordered breakfast. Thank God, he was thinking, thank God he had a good appetite. He was going to need it.

He ate steak and eggs and spuds and drank lots of coffee. He figured he must have eaten two meals. Then he went down to the barbershop, where he found the old man just opening up.

"I want a real hot tub," he said. "And I want you to stay in my sight while I take it."

After his bath and a good soaking of his gun arm, he went to Carrigan's and bought a whole new rig and extra ammunition. His hope was that they had not taken the buckskin or any of his saddle rigging. He had hidden his weapons.

The hostler wasn't around when he came in, but he heard him up in the loft forking hay down to the horses below. He checked the buckskin and saw that he was all right. Being an Indian pony, he didn't have shoes, and that was fine with Slocum. Then he waited until he heard the hostler moving to the far end of the loft, and climbed up the wall ladder and felt around in the pile of hay where he had cached his Sharps, the Greener .12-gauge, and his possibles bag. He managed to drop back down to the buckskin's stall without the hostler noticing him. By the time the man got back down, Slocum had already ridden out.

But he knew they were following him. And he was sure they'd have men along the trail up ahead to box him in whenever they figured it was a right time.

Once again he rode the high ground, checking his back trail often and thoroughly. This, of course, meant he couldn't cover much ground. But he felt safer. They were following him, he knew. The point was to play them; not let them get too close, and not too far behind; and to try to throw them off when the right moment came. So he headed east out of town, riding deliberately in a direction that would take him to the cabin where Jeremy and Dora Patches were waiting for him.

He was counting on whoever was following him to figure he was making a false start. They would realize that he knew he was being followed and so would try to fool them. Then later, when he broke away from the trail, the trackers would take it that he was now heading for his true destination. But he would be doing just the opposite.

Slocum knew their weakness. He had learned much from the Indians, and he had verified all of it. He knew how impatient the whites were—with some exceptions, such as the old mountain men and some of the trappers, but there were few of them around. Being impatient, a man didn't take pains. He hurried, and always had his eye on the goal instead of on the means of getting there; that is, on the present. Somehow most of the men coming into the West, good men and bad, were concerned with gain of one sort or another: cattle, gold, land, power; it was all the same. They took and took and seldom had the time for contacting what was actually going on in the land or with another person or an animal, or even the weather. There were exceptions; Jeremy Patches was one. But Jeremy was fighting a losing fight. Maybe his old friend would die, but Slocum knew he would die with honor; yes, with unsung honor. The best kind.

In the late afternoon he cut down a hard, long-unused game trail, but walking his unshod pony along the side of the slender track, and dismounting and returning on foot to make certain he had left no sign. He repeated this operation a few times until he was sure he had eluded the men who were following him, and that he had left no back trail.

Then all at once he smelled it again. It came wafting in to him as the slight wind shifted and he rode down toward the copse of cottonwood trees. Overhead he saw a buzzard circling. There was no question where he was. The sign was still there, and the old, rotted ropes dangling from the branches. But there was one thing different.

From the branch of the big cottonwood a fresh body was hanging. Slocum rode right up to it, thinking the man might miraculously be alive. But he was soon shed of such a notion. The face was swollen, and had been picked at by a vulture, and the eyes had popped out. There was no question that the hanging had been recent. Perhaps within the past two days. Slocum did not recognize the man, but he could read the sign pinned to his shirt:

Another Hors Theef
pays th price
signed COURTESY THE SOCIETY FOR THE
DISCOURAGEMENT OF HORSE THIEVING,
ROBBERY AND KILLING

He remembered hearing in the Pastime back in Rock Creek only a day ago that the gang that had shot up the town and killed five people had been located and the vigilantes were closing in on them.

Was this really a horse thief? Or was he just some poor fool who had a crime pinned on him for convenience?

Slocum didn't let his thoughts stay him from his purpose. He kicked the buckskin into a brisk canter and soon the hanging tree and its fresh decoration were well behind him.

He was within sight of Franc's Peak now, and his back trail was clear, but Jeremy and Dora were going to have to wait. He had a more pressing matter to deal with before he saw them. He was pretty close now, and he knew that if he wanted he could let the buckskin have his head. But he also knew he was taking one huge risk.

A man in his right mind wouldn't dream of riding into a hostile Indian camp with a horse that belonged to the tribe. Especially when it was a camp he'd just escaped from. But Slocum wanted to know something. He knew if he went to the Indian agent he wouldn't get a straight answer. He also knew he might get killed—or worse—riding into the Arapaho camp like this. But he knew too that the Indians took boldness and courage into account. It was something nobody else would do, and they would know that. And so he would do it. And it had damn well better work.

8

Jeremy Patches was sitting up on his bed, which lay flat on the floor of the cabin, and had begun filling his pipe. He was a man of deliberation, usually taking his time to turn things over before deciding, and moving slowly; except when necessary, when he could move as fast as any. But his way was slow. He would have made a great sheepherder, John Slocum thought at one point, but had the good sense never to mention it to Jeremy. Jeremy was a cattleman through and through.

He had fought and bled for his land down where the JP had been. First finding a place that was nigh inaccessible to strangers, then building everything himself. Then saving, scrimping, finally getting a small herd together. Grace had been all the help he wanted. But then Dora had come. And he'd had to go it alone. Nobody wanted to come all the way up on that mountain to help a man build his spread with nothing around but the seasons. So he'd gone it alone.

Now and then he'd left the ranch for a spell, when Dora was old enough and Grace could handle things, and had hired out to the big spreads around the country. That way he built a little savings and also got some more cattle; it being the custom then for the small cattlemen—for that matter, the big ones too—to throw their own brand on any slicks they came across—stray calves with no mother about and no brand. The big men did it, and the little men did it too. The difference was, the big men got away with it; the small stockmen were soon ostracized by the big outfits. Finally, when land became scarce and water rights a problem, the small stockmen became the target for attack by the Association.

One day the small cattlemen banded together and started their own association. The result of this was the big cattle war which the small stockmen won, thanks largely to men like Jeremy Patches. But the victory had weakened all of them. They didn't have the resources for recovery that the big men had. The Stockgrowers Association was still there, and so were the "regulators" and cattle detectives and hired gunmen. Money still called the turn.

Then Grace had caught sick and died. Dora had been teaching school in Rock Creek, but now Jeremy called her home and together they'd been running the ranch for two years when Slocum showed up.

He was damn glad now that Slocum had answered his letter, for it had gotten worse than the cattle war, this new push to take his ranch. He wasn't even sure who was behind it. No cattle were stolen—not yet, anyway. But his water had been damned up more than once, some cattle had been hazed off his land, and when he'd found them mixed in with Tandry's stock or Clem Newhouse's, those gentlemen had been most ungracious, and a couple of times their foremen had even been threatening. They were being careful because of the new law that had settled the cattle war in favor of the small stockmen, but they were still putting on the pressure. Then his herd began to dwindle; slowly, but still it was getting smaller.

Clem Newhouse had offered to buy him out as a "friendly gesture from a neighbor," and Jeremy had told him to get the hell off JP land, and right now. And then some cows had been shot, a horse stolen right out of his pasture.

And then one morning at dawn he heard the horsemen. He was up and out to meet them. Billy Dime and his boys, all of them, had been riders for the Association. And the next thing he saw after looking them over was the sorrel stallion in his round horse corral.

"We are arresting you for horse stealing, Patches," Dime had told him.

Thank God Dora had been away overnight in town, for Jeremy had ducked back into the cabin and come up with his Sharps and blasted those half-dozen horsemen right out of his sight. He hadn't aimed to kill, but to scare. And he'd got rid of them. But he knew that was only for the moment. It was then he wrote to Slocum.

Over the years they'd kept a slim contact, neither one being a letter writer, but both had mutual acquaintances who relayed messages. Jeremy would never forget that spring when he'd been flat busted broke and Slocum had worked with him running in mustangs and breaking them for the army so he could make a stake. Nor would he ever forget Slocum's help in the cattle war.

When they'd burned his ranch it got to him. And on top of that he had this game leg. He still had the hunting cabin up by Franc's Peak. But he'd not been able to transport his arsenal of dynamite, three sawed-down shotguns, an extra Spencer and Henry, two Navy Colts with hair-balance, and all the ammunition he could fit into that fake outhouse all but totally concealed in the pine and spruce above the ranch. It was a regular outhouse, and the buried arsenal was covered by a two-holer. But it was still down at the ranch, and not easy to come on. Just an innocent-looking old shack. He had thought to have Dora start packing the weapons and ammo up to the cabin, but it was a heavy job and he was afraid there'd be men watching the place.

He wished Slocum would return. Slocum could get the guns and ammo and the dynamite. He began to wonder about his leg. It had started throbbing again. But he put the thought of it out of his mind and when the door of the cabin opened and Dora came in he was smiling at her.

Immediately he saw that something was wrong.

"What is it, honey?"

"I'm pretty sure there's somebody watching the cabin."

Instinctively Jeremy reached out his hand to touch the Winchester that was lying on the blankets beside him.

"Stay in, then," he said. "Did they see you?"

"I don't know."

"But what sign did you see?"

"I didn't see anything. I just had that feeling. I still do."

"Then don't go out. It'll be dark soon. Maybe I'll slip out then for a little look-see."

She had shaken her worry then and was smiling. "No, you're not going anywhere. You're going to stay right in bed until your leg is better."

"Throw that extra bar across the door," he said.

The times were hard. It was especially the old people who said so. And at the same time, the young men were restless, eager to hunt, to earn honors and count coup on an enemy. But now there were no enemies, and little hunting.

There had been no fighting with the white soldiers for a long while. And now there was the poisoning with the pieces of fat the white men put out to catch the wolves. A dog had eaten some, and Old Tomahawk had too. They had gotten sick; not so bad, but it could have been worse.

It was the end of the Moon of New Buds and the Arapahoes, only two sleeps away from the white soldiers, were at peace. With the moon growing again, the land awakening in the summertime, the people were wishing for a big hunt. But the white man had forbidden it; the white men said there would be the food given. And, again, the thing that had been said was not so. Many days had passed from the time that it was for the food to be given from the white men's wagons. And the pots were still empty, the cook fires not flaming.

Blue Cloud watched and listened. He did not know how to ease the restlessness of the young warriors, especially when the white men brought the whiskey wagons and the young men drank the burning brown water. This day Blue Cloud had watched the light breaking gently over the Arapaho camp, the sun slipping across the tops of the tepees, resting so briefly on the cottonwood and crackwillow in the draws that ran through the surrounding prairie. Much of the rolling prairie was greening, but it would not do so for long. Soon the rolling green grass would turn brown, the familiar leather-colored stalks knitting the earth's cover. And next year . . . And next year, the old ones predicted, there would be less buffalo, less game to fill the parfleches. If only they could all go on a big hunt, as in the old days . . .

In the lodge of Blue Cloud, half a dozen headmen sat with their chief. This was the council. Each one had entered the lodge carefully, paying attention to everything necessary for the occasion and the person of he who had led them since the time of Many Horses Running. They had seated themselves in the correct order—each had his place—and had smoked, passing the pipe around the circle in the prescribed manner.

When the pipe had been smoked, Blue Cloud placed it carefully in the special place on the robe in front of him.

"It is well to speak," Blue Cloud said. "There is the whiskey still and it is being traded more, and I hear now that some is being given."

"Given?" an older man named Mole spoke the word harshly.

"It is so," the chief said. "Runs Quickly and Weasel saw it. They could do nothing."

"The camp police must be told," said another elder.

"It has been done." Blue Cloud said the words softly, yet they carried to all ears in the lodge. "All has been done that can be done. They have drunk too much, those who accepted the whiskey, and now they are sick. I have ordered the camp police to pony whip them when they have become themselves again. But something more lasting must be done."

"Why are the whites giving whiskey?" an elder named Looks Twice asked.

"That is why we are in council," Blue Cloud said. "And why did somebody steal a horse from the pony herd? It was one of the drinkers who gave it for the whiskey. That is what I have been told."

"It is Singing Man's horse, and he should whip the thief."

"Aah . . ." another said. "Then it was not the white man."

"Slo-come. No. He was at the Wood River," Blue Cloud said. "He helped us. He is not one to steal."

"Then why did you not let him go?" Mole asked. "And he escaped."

"At first I did not know he was the same one who was at Wood River and helped Many Horses Running. Nor did anyone know a whiskey warrior had stolen the pony. When I was told, he had already escaped. I did not send warriors after him."

"So it was one with the whiskey. . ."

"He will be punished."

"*Ho* . . ." the others said in agreement. "It is so."

Now a warrior named Bad Face spoke. "But why are the whites giving whiskey? Trading, yes; as with the pony. But to give. It is something to fear, that. From the white man. To give means he will want a hundred times more than what was given."

"*Heya*," said the others.

Bad Face spoke again. "The whites are coming more swiftly than the grass in the spring, and they are more than the blades of grass that cover the prairie."

"And what of the agent man?" asked a warrior who had not yet spoken. He was a thickset man with a large scar running down the left side of his face. His name was Old Smoke.

"It was this too why the council was called," Blue Cloud said. He leaned forward and lifted the pipe from its special place and began preparing it again. All were silent, deep in thought. Presently, when the pipe was ready, they smoked.

When it was done Blue Cloud said, "The agent man says we must move from here."

"Move our village?" Bad Face said. "But to where?"

"Clearly, it will be some place the *Wasichus* do not want," said Looks Twice.

"I do not know where." Blue Cloud said. He looked across the circle to a warrior who had not yet spoken. "Many Sleeps was there. Tell what you saw."

"The agent man was afraid," Many Sleeps said. "He had been drinking the whiskey."

"As always," said Mole.

"What can be done?" Bad Face asked.

A warrior named Two Horns now spoke for the first time. "There is nothing to be done. Yes, we can fight and all be killed. That could be better than to live as they want us to live. But if we are all killed, what will happen to the people?" He was an old man and his voice was sad.

"It is so," Blue Cloud said. "We saw many soldiers on our way to the agent man."

"We must fight them," said Bad Face, "or they will kill us all."

A long silence fell.

At last Blue Cloud spoke. He was not the oldest in the circle, but he was no longer a young man; and he was one to whom all in the tribe listened. He was no paper chief, appointed by the whites to run things as they wished.

"It is important to remember that the white man does not fight as the Arapahoes or Sioux or any of the people of the land. They wish to destroy everything. But we must survive. It is only important that our people live. If we fight them they will kill us all, and our nation will be no more."

These words fell heavily into the lodge and there followed a long silence.

When the warriors had left the lodge, Blue Cloud took his own pipe from its rabbit fur pouch and filled it. Then, offering it to the four directions, and to The Above, he prayed.

All during the night he sat in his blanket, not moving, not even when one of his wives brought him food. For these days there was much to disturb the heart—the young men wanting to fight the whites, and now in anger taking to the burning water. He knew that only he and a dwindling few of the older ones stood between an open break with the soldier men. Blue Cloud had fought the pony soldiers and had defeated them too, and he did not fear them. But to be destroyed completely, or to bow the head and accept slavery? It was not an easy choice, not with the women and children and the old ones to care for. What would happen to them if all fought to the death? Who would care for the babes still suckling at their mothers' breasts?

It was much trouble. His heart had never been so heavy. Well, he would go to a high place and build a lodge and purify himself with the heat from the fire that would be specially built. He would then cry for a vision; he would dream. For as he was he still could not see. And it was necessary to see what was the good way for the people. For this he needed help from what was Above.

All night he sat in his lodge, and at the time of the morning star in the eastern sky he felt something in him. The sun was just at the horizon when a messenger came to tell him that the white man who had escaped had returned.

It was the feeling he knew so well, even though it was anything but common. That strange sweeping that claimed him when he was coming into a special danger. It was the feeling that nothing really mattered, that what was going to happen was going to happen, and everything would be as it was going to be—Yes, lawful was the word that always came.

And this was especially so now, as he rode round the high cutbank at the creek, and there in the box elders, cottonwoods, and willows lay the Arapaho camp. He knew they were expecting him, that Blue Cloud was expecting him. He didn't know how he knew it, and it didn't matter. He knew.

Now, unaccompanied by angry guards as he had been on his previous visit, he was more free to take in the panorama. The exquisite dancing of the first sunlight on the thick goldenrod, the smoke rising from the lodge smoke holes, the grazing bells tinkling in the pony herd, all evoked something that was unnameable, something that required no explanation as far as Slocum was concerned.

The lodges were set in the usual horseshoe, with the opening toward the rising sun. There were darting bluebirds and yellow flowers everywhere, but no game that could be seen. But mostly, there were no buffalo chips, and he noticed that the bark on the trees had not been rubbed off by the buffalo scratching themselves. It was just one more sign of the swift disappearance of the great herds.

The camp was unusually still as Slocum rode in. A few of the men who happened to be in sight stood watching him, staring boldly with no expression on their faces. The women were stone.

Chief Blue Cloud was still seated on the buffalo robe in front of the low fire of buffalo chips when Slocum was escorted into his lodge.

Without a word Slocum took the place that had been prepared for him opposite the chief.

The Arapaho chief now filled the traditional pipe and lighted it with a small chip which he lifted from the fire. He passed it to Slocum, and they smoked in silence for several moments.

At length the Indian said, "Now we can speak with words that come straight from the heart. For we have smoked, and one cannot lie when one has smoked."

"You told Blue Cloud then." These words were spoken by Henry Skinner directly at A. B. Howser, the Indian Agent for the Arapahoes.

Howser, a very fat man with a full beard that did not entirely hide his bulging neck, nodded. Even though it wasn't very hot, he was sweating. He always did whenever he had to talk with Henry Skinner or any of his superiors in the government, or high rankers in the army; not to mention the Indians. Only with small children was he able to handle himself without the timidity that had been the abiding feature of his life of some fifty years.

"Told him straight out they might likely have to move."

"But you didn't say it definitely!"

A.B. nodded, hoping he'd done the right thing. "You said to imply, I do believe."

"That is correct." Skinner was seated in the agent's cabin facing A.B., and leaning his elbows on the arms of his rickety chair he began to massage his temples with his fingertips. "Good, then." He nodded. "Yes, imply to them, and let *them* make it definite."

"There was a big foofaraw about that Appaloosa horse. The Araps hauled in that feller Slocum, claiming he'd stole it; well, it sure looked like it since he was riding the animal, though he'd hired it from Morgan's livery in Rock Creek." A.B. reached for the bottle and poured a second round for himself and company.

"Where is Slocum now?"

"Dunno. He busted out of the camp, got clean away. So my scout tells me."

"Howser, I want to tell you something." Skinner had stopped massaging his temples and now sat absolutely still regarding the Arapaho agent. "I have heard, and from what you tell me too, that the Araps are pretty damn restless. Good. The delay on their rations has helped, and so has the whiskey, and so has their not knowing what's going to happen. I'm talking about the hints you've been dropping, followed now by something more sure. It's good," he said, leaning back and slapping his knee lightly. He watched the smile lighting A.B's moonlike face. "It's good." And then he added, "But it is *not good enough!*" And he watched the fat man's face fall.

"Hell, Henry, I done all I can, I mean without getting kicked out of my job. I've done exactly what you been telling me. Dropping hints, delaying things. I figure you want them uncertain so's they'll take to leaving for a new camp better than if things were real good here an' they didn't want to go. That right? Am I right there?" His voice rose.

Henry Skinner smiled. He had A.B. where he wanted him. Hungry. Eager. Fearful. "Not too bad," he said. "But there is something else."

He waited, watching Howser's eyes wandering around the little office in his cabin, not knowing where to look. "There is Jeremy Patches's place."

Puzzlement settled into A.B's creamy gaze. He didn't have very much hair on top of his head, yet he still swept his fingers through it in an agitated gesture. Skinner had taken note of how often he did this.

"I don't get the connection, Henry. Sorry."

"The connection is that Patches's JP is the block of land that connects two large sections up above Jack Creek; that is to say, it *could* connect, but at the moment, as it is now, it *separates* these two large sections which, taken all together—including the JP—would be an excellent location for the Arapahoes."

He saw the puzzlement in the other man's face turn to enlightenment, and he hoped he had said the right thing. He hoped he hadn't shown his hand too soon. But the deal was closing in, and he needed Howser in a stronger position. Commitment would do it if anything would.

"But there's nothing there," A.B. said, looking stupid. "Outside of Patches's outfit, those rocks and gumbo aren't going to offer anything for a tribe of Indians."

"It'll be temporary," Skinner said swiftly. "I know it's not the greatest choice, but the people I represent are adamant about obtaining the present Arapaho land. Let me put it like that. The Arapahoes can be moved again."

"They won't like that," A.B. said weakly.

"They don't have such a great package of land as it is now. Maybe later something better could turn up."

"When would this take place, Henry?"

"Soon."

"How soon? Could you give me a notion?"

"Very soon. It is a situation that must be kept absolutely secret. Do you understand?"

A.B. Howser nodded quickly, his eyes opening wide as it began to sink further in.

"It is something that comes from . . . well, let me say, from back East." And he looked at his man closely, allowing his loaded words to have their effect.

"I take it very few know of this," A.B. said cagily.

"You and I know," Skinner said, his eyes hard on the other man. "That's all we need to understand, Howser."

His use of A.B's last name nailed it, he could see.

"What do you want me to do, Henry?"

"I want you to play this very close. We want the Araps to be docile, you understand? No trouble. At the same time, we've been spreading rumors that they might not be so docile and this is another reason for moving them. Where they are now they're trouble: buying whiskey, guns, and maybe even getting ready for some raiding parties. I don't want any soft-hearts in Rock Creek or Tilghman's or in Washington especially to feel the poor little old Injuns is gettin' a raw deal. And I certainly do not want any interference from the army. The army will be handled from back East. What we're dealing with is people's feelings. I want everybody to *want* the Arapahoes to move off that land, and the only place they can move to is the area by Jack Creek and Stone Basin."

They were silent for a long moment, and Skinner could tell what Howser was thinking. The man was like a great big child, he told himself; you could read him like a book.

"You're wondering why?" he said suddenly.

A.B. flushed all over his big head, his neck, and, it seemed to Henry Skinner, especially his ears. He wondered how the man had ever gotten to be an Indian agent. Of course, he wasn't the first incompetent to be put into such a job.

Howser sniffed, sighed, and said, "Matter of fact, that is just what I was wondering, Henry." He hiccuped suddenly. "Looks like somebody just wants that land real bad."

"I reckon it could look like that," Skinner said, standing up and lifting his glass to finish his drink. "You know you're just following orders. Right? So keep alert. When Blue Cloud or any of them question you, you don't know anything, but you'll try to find out." Henry Skinner raised his eyes to look out the window. He could see some blue flowers and he wondered if Howser had planted them. But he didn't let the thought go any further. Striding to the door and the horse and gig he had driven out from town, he said, "Only one thing standing in our way."

"Patches."

"Patches." Skinner stood in the open doorway and faced back to A.B., who had followed slowly after him. "Once we get Patches's land then the boys back East can arrange the moving of the Araps. And I think it's about time now."

"But just where the hell is Patches?" A.B. asked.

"Looks like he's disappeared. D'you reckon he's left the country?"

"He is not the type to run. But I have trackers after him. So far Slocum hasn't led us anywhere," he went on sourly, "except up the garden path."

"Arapahoes?" Howser asked, suddenly aware of his charges and his responsibilities toward them.

"Shoshone." Skinner grinned wickedly. "Don't get your ass in an uproar, Howser."

"They're good trackers."

"They're good trackers if they find—*when* they find Jeremy Patches. And only then."

He stepped into the gig then and took the reins. "You know where to find me if you need to. But remember to be careful. We don't want to be seen together."

A.B. watched him all the way out of sight. He was still watching after Henry Skinner when the arrow entered his back, pierced his lung, and killed him.

9

"So it was you!" Dora cried when she opened the cabin door to admit Slocum.

"Who were you expecting?" he said with a laugh, happy and relieved to see her and Jeremy, who was standing at one of the windows with his Winchester ready.

"Dora heard—or felt—somebody out there. It was you, I hope," Jeremy said with a grin while Dora slid the bar back across the door.

"It was me. I checked around before coming in, and there *has* been somebody watching the place. I'm pretty sure it was another Shoshone, maybe looking for his friend. But I think it's time to get out of here."

"D'you mean that?" the girl asked in alarm. "You expect trouble?"

"Not this minute maybe, but soon enough. Say, how about some coffee?"

"How about something to eat? Have you et?" Jeremy had drawn up a chair and pointed to another one for Slocum to sit in while Dora got something together at the stove.

"So tell what's happened," Jeremy said. "Nothing's happened here. My leg's just about the way it ought to be. So I'll be ready for those buggers any time, any place."

"That might be pretty soon now," Slocum said seriously. "I had a good talk with Blue Cloud. It looks like somebody's really aiming to get them moved."

"Moved? Why? They been making trouble for the ranchers, or what? Hell, it wouldn't be anything new."

"Not that," Slocum said, smiling up at Dora as she handed him a mug of steaming coffee. He sniffed loudly. "By golly, that game smells real good."

"And it'll taste good, I hope," she said, returning to the stove, with a happy laugh.

Slocum tore his eyes away from her and looked at Jeremy. "I don't believe the Arapahoes have been making any trouble at all, but I have evidence that somebody has been fixing it to look that way."

"But why? You mean, somebody wants them off that land where they are now badly enough to make it look like they're fixing to cause trouble? You mean like painting up and hitting the path?"

Slocum nodded, leaning forward in his chair with his coffee mug in his two hands. He took a pull at the hot coffee and sighed with pleasure. "Your daughter really makes good Arbuckle, my friend."

They chuckled at that.

"Wait'll you taste this steak," said the girl at the stove.

"We can't wait," Slocum said with a grin. Then he

was serious again. "Somebody—and it's got to be somebody big—really wants that land. Blue Cloud opened up with me. He's worried. He told me they discovered some men recently, whites, with instruments that sure sound to me like surveying stuff."

"But they've got a treaty. They don't have to move."

"They'll have to move if the army is called in on account of their making trouble, raiding and all that. I've got a strong notion that there'll be some Indian raids, but my question will be—what Indians?"

"You mean, maybe whites?"

"Just after I left Blue Cloud I heard the agent—Howser, you likely know him—was killed right outside his cabin. They found him with an Arapaho arrow sticking in his back. I can't prove it, but I know that wasn't one of Blue Cloud's people. Not unless he was drunk as a jaybird! But the Arapahoes will be blamed."

Jeremy ran the palm of his hand across his forehead. "Brother!" He shook his head solemnly. "So you reckon there's maybe gold."

"That's what it begins to look like. Gold or silver, or both maybe."

"Anybody know about this?"

"I'd say you and me and Dora and whoever it is who's working like a dog to get those Arapahoes the hell off that land."

"But where will the army or the government put the Arapahoes then, if they move them from where they are now?" Dora asked, placing the loaded plates on the table.

"You guessed it," Jeremy said, catching Slocum's eyes on him. "You've got one guess and the first two don't count."

"That land around your outfit, Jeremy, that's government land, is it?"

"Nobody else would want it. And the JP splits it right down, almost down the middle. So I guess some smart feller is figuring to get it all in one block and shove it up—excuse me—*down* the red man's throat." He beamed at Dora for his near slip of the tongue, but Slocum could see there was no real humor in it.

The girl had come back to the table now with her own plate of food and sat down with them. "But is that true, John? Can that really happen?" She was staring at him in astonishment.

"It makes too much sense from a certain angle to be anything *but* true," Slocum said. "I'm afraid it is true. Everything is explained by that—their wanting your place, the rash of robberies, the effort of the vigilantes to take over the law, the whiskey being given—not sold but given—to the Indians, and the guns too. And especially A.B. Howser's murder. Next move will be the army coming in and either killing all of them or moving them. So where will they move them?"

"Neat." Jeremy picked up his knife and fork and repeated himself. "Neat."

Slocum didn't linger after his meal with Dora and Jeremy Patches. He would have liked nothing better than to remain a long, long time in the presence of that lovely girl, but this was no time for pleasure. So he told them he was going to back track whoever had been watching the cabin for the past two days and see what he could discover.

He was pretty sure it was another Shoshone, and as he now worked his way along the man's trail he became certain it was no white man and no Arapaho.

He had the definite feeling that something was about to break, as he had told the Patches, warning them to stay inside the cabin and do nothing until his return. One thing that worried him too was the obvious fact that while Jeremy was putting on a brave front, his leg had still not mended. He had told him so. "You need rest, because we're going to have to go back down to the ranch pretty soon now; or, at any rate, get out of here. That's two visitors too many have been up here." With that he had left them.

The talk with Blue Cloud had revealed a lot. He'd only had time to give Jeremy and the girl the highlights. But he had definitely struck the right note of bravado by riding back into the Arapaho camp.

Indeed, he had struck such an accord with Blue Cloud that the chief insisted he keep the buckskin horse Yellow Feather had gotten him, though he apparently knew nothing of her role in Slocum's escape. At any rate, he was saying nothing about it.

Slocum was sure from the description that the men with the "looking eyes" and poles were surveyors; and he could think of no reason why there would be any surveying on that particular strip of land unless it was in relation to mining. Surely no railroad could ever get through to any good purpose.

He had parted with the chief on the best terms, Blue Cloud appreciating the fact that Slocum knew how to be without the white man's arrogance, as he put it.

"You speak like man," he had said. "Not treat Indian like dirt."

"I am friend of the Arapaho," Slocum had said. "I will try to help you."

And when they parted the chief had given him a small package wrapped in soft leather. "You keep this with you, Slo-cum. Remember it will give you power."

Later, when he had stopped along the trail to open it, he found a pure white stone. The stone, more than any words, told him that Blue Cloud would be ready to do whatever was necessary.

It had not been easy following the trail of the man who had been watching the cabin. And Slocum was more and more certain that the quicker the Patches got out of there the safer they would be. It would be only a very short while before others knew where Jeremy was.

He was now coming into the country close to Jeremy's JP, still the rough country of rocks and timber, and on the side of the mountain that faced toward Rock Creek. On the other side the land was more open. There was grass and sweeping prairie and meadows, good country for grazing stock, which was where the cattlemen ran their beeves during the summer. And there were also the mines. But on this side of the mountain where he now was, there was little feed and the trail was rough. Only the area where Jeremy had started his herd could afford even a few head of cattle. As he looked at the land, Slocum realized more fully that the only reason Jeremy had come up here was for the solitude and the contact with the land and the sky.

He was riding along a rocky trail. The Indian's tracks had given out, but Slocum still could feel his way. He knew somehow that this was the way the Indian had come. It was the only way that made trail sense.

Then all at once at a turn in the trail he came to the edge of a high bluff, fringed with pine and spruce, with a vista below of a series of box canyons. For a moment it looked like a collection of squares and oblongs cut out of rocks and earth; but a place where the easiest thing in the world would have been to get lost. And there, almost directly below him, he saw something glittering in the sunlight.

Two hours later he had descended to the rim of the actual canyon, a three-sided "box" with an opening through which horses could be driven, or cattle, and held, the terrain affording a natural corral. These canyons were often used for wrangling wild horses and breaking them. In fact, he and Jeremy had done just that, not very far from where he was now.

Careful to remain well hidden, he had dismounted and had crept closer to the edge of the canyon from which he had caught the glinting of something or other. As he got down closer he could smell the campfire. Rounding a sharp turn in the overgrown trail he'd been following, he suddenly saw a big remuda of horses grazing in a lush meadow. At the far end of the meadow he saw some corrals and what in a moment he realized was a large log cabin.

It was early evening and there were cookfires and men eating. There must have been thirty men there, and at least double that amount of horses.

He had crept as close as he dared now, studying the camp through his field glasses.

It had to be Mysterious Billy's boys. He had no doubt of that, and his suspicion was verified shortly when he saw the gentleman himself airing his views to a small group of slouching, grinning desperadoes. It was a type he knew well. The War had taught him all he needed to know about men—the good and the bad, and the nondescript; and, too, the special.

He didn't dare come closer, so it was not possible to hear any of the conversations, save for a few shouts. There was obviously drinking going on. But he was concerned about getting out now. He had seen no outriders coming in, but of course he hadn't entered the box canyon through its lone opening, but had come over the top and down through scrub oak, pine, rock, and thick brush. Getting back, however, wasn't going to be so easy. It was just then he spotted the shiny black gig and the dappled mare he'd seen outside Teddy's.

The sun was down behind the high ground now as he started back up to where he had left the buckskin. The air was cooler, but he was still hot from his effort to keep hidden. It took a good two hours to get back to where he had left his horse. He rode away under a velvet sky, wondering who owned that gig and what the person had been doing at Teddy's; glad too that he had found Mysterious Billy's headquarters, but at the same time with a grim feeling of the tremendous odds that were stacked against himself and Jeremy and Dora. Sure, Blue Cloud would help, however he could, but Slocum had seen thirty tough gunmen down there in that box canyon, and he had seen the racks of rifles, ready like an army, the good horseflesh, and he knew the determination of a man such as Mysterious Billy Dime, who would stop nowhere until he reached what he wanted and had to have.

The question that was bothering him the most now was when. He had no doubt as to their plan. They would simply take over the ranch now that no one was there. It was deserted, wasn't it? Patches had left, probably left the country for good. Simple. Why hadn't he thought of that sooner? Well, he hadn't. But he could tell just as sure as whoever it was up there who made those little apples—that it was going to be soon. Something in the way the men were, the loudly confident atmosphere, the feel of that deadly camp, told him that it would be soon.

It was still evening as he reached the flat land, and there was light in the sky. Now that the mountains had dropped slightly away, as it were, the horizon receding, he was able to see for some distance. Up ahead he was sure he could make out a horse and gig with a single driver. At least from this distance it looked like the same gig he had seen in the canyon. It could easily be the same. There was one way to find out. The only thing he had to be sure of was to keep from being spotted either by the driver of the gig or by any possible outriders of Mysterious Billy Dime's. He had an idea who might be driving that gig; it certainly wasn't any cow waddie. He wanted to see who it was. And besides that, he wanted to see T. P. Daventry.

It took less time to reach Rock Creek coming from Billy Dime's box canyon than it did from the JP, and he managed to keep in good range of the horse and gig. By now he remembered the night he'd seen the spanking dappled mare and the shiny gig outside Teddy's Palace de Joy, the same night he'd spotted Mysterious Billy's big bay horse.

Was it Skinner in the gig?

He'd heard that Skinner had money in the Palace de Joy. Did he run it? And how deeply was Teddy associated with Mysterious Billy Dime? She had to be connected somehow or other, for she'd sent the cardplayers all packing that night when the baldheaded bartender had come in with his message. But was Teddy also in on the Indian removal plan?

His thoughts turned to the cardplayers—the whiskey train men and Preacher Tom Thompson. Were they all connected, all working together on the Arapaho deal? Somehow he wouldn't have picked Teddy for that kind of action. She seemed strictly gaming—cards, dice, the wheel. But of course you never knew. You never knew about women, you never knew about gamblers, hell, you never knew people.

He watched the dappled grey mare and the gig stop at the big house outside Rock Creek, and waited while the man descended. Yes, from the description he'd heard of Skinner from Ginger it had to be him.

In just a short while he had ridden into town and hitched the buckskin outside the sheriff's office. He figured the sheriff's hitching rail would be safer than the livery where the Appaloosa had been passed off on him. He'd settle that score later.

Slocum felt lucky, and he was. Though the office was locked, he saw the sheriff just coming into sight from making his first evening rounds.

"Looking for me, are you?" T. P. spoke around the cigarette he was holding in his mouth, squinting some.

Slocum realized that with his glass eye he shouldn't have to squint against the smoke, yet he did.

"Like to have a word with you," he said as Daventry opened the door and went in, leaving it open behind him for his visitor.

"Likewise," T.P. said, but nodding toward Slocum, who then told him what he had seen out at the box canyon, and how he had followed Henry Skinner into town.

"And I heard about Ansel Howser," he said.

"Ansel got shot with a arrow by—it looks like—one of Blue Cloud's band."

"I'd like to see the body," Slocum said.

"Down to Doc Traynor's. Help yourself." He squinted. "You got a suspicion on something?"

"Maybe." Slocum stood up. "Come on down with

me. I'll tell you about my visit with Blue Cloud."

The sheriff's eyebrows shot up at that. "I heard you got captured for horse stealing." He grinned as he stood up and adjusted his Stetson hat. "News gets about. It's like the weather, ain't it? Everybody gets it sooner or later."

At Doc Traynor's they found A.B. lying on a bench, which had been especially built for the purpose. A new pine box, just constructed by E. L. Waters, the town carpenter, stood waiting on two trestles. The burial, T.P. informed Slocum, would be in the morning. A.B. had no kin out in this country, and no one knew anything else about him.

Slocum was only half listening, as he looked down at the body. "Where is the arrow?" he asked.

Doc walked over to some clothing in a corner of the room that had evidently been A.B's. In a moment he was back, holding the arrow. "Here's what I dug out of him," he said.

Slocum took the shaft and examined it. "It's not an Arapaho arrow," he said.

T.P. pursed his lips, lifted his eyebrows, and sniffed, but said nothing.

"See those markings?" Slocum pointed to the colored marks right near the end of the arrow where it was notched. "They're not Arapaho. I don't know what tribe they are. I don't think any. I'd say a white man shot that arrow and wanted it to look like an Indian had done it." He looked directly at Daventry. "It wouldn't be the first time."

When they got back to the sheriff's office, Slocum recounted his talk with Blue Cloud. When he was finished they both fell silent for some time, each turning the situation over in his thoughts.

At last T. P. Daventry said, "What you figure is their next move?"

"I dunno. I expect 'em to move in on the JP with that army they've got out at the box canyon. But just when that'll be I don't know."

"You're saying they'll take the place because it's deserted."

"That'll be their excuse. Not that they need one."

"They'll still need something to get around the law," the sheriff said grimly.

"They have got something, Daventry. They have got a whole arsenal of guns out there and they've got the men to shoot them."

T. P. Daventry stood up and hitched up his pants, checked the hang of his holstered gun, and said, "It ain't time yet, but think I'll make my rounds again."

"And I got to get out to the JP."

They stepped out onto the boardwalk together, each checking the street swiftly.

"Slocum, you still not aiming to work with me?"

"That is correct, Sheriff."

T. P. Daventry, his eyes still on the street, nodded. "Good enough. Might run into you up around Jack Creek." And, still without looking at Slocum, he started along the boardwalk.

Slocum liked a man who didn't waste his time.

Sunny Jim had been feeling anything but sunny this day and so Preacher Tom Thompson had prescribed his famous All-Over Cure-All. The result was so immediately rewarding to the doleful Jim that both Saginaw BiLl Lavigne and Charlie O'Moss had followed suit, having decided that they too were not quite up to the mark. Particularly in view of the fact that High-Queen

Teddy had called a meeting with the four of them, all felt the need for support. Preacher himself had already sampled his product, as he did each morning to make sure it had not deteriorated. He considered this morning ritual as a duty to his customers. Preacher knew himself as a man of honor, and in fact, even went so far as to check his fabulous elixir a few more times during the day, not to mention the evening.

"It's important to insist on high quality," he told his companions as they sat in their wagon for a moment before entering the Palace de Joy.

"What do you reckon the old bitch wants?" Charlie O'Moss asked. "It ain't like her to 'call a meeting.' What the hell's she up to?"

"Up to no good, you can bet your sweet petunia," Saginaw Bill observed.

Sunny Jim beamed on his companions, totally recovered from his morning indisposition. "One way to find out," he said with a brisk laugh. Feeling really good, he snapped each of his suspenders in succession. Charlie O'Moss, seated on the edge of the wagon box, almost fell into the street, he began laughing so hard.

It was Preacher Tom, though, who had his eye on the seriousness of the moment. "Time to get inside, I reckon," he said, and began climbing down from the wagon seat.

The cool gloom of the saloon at midday was a pleasant relief from the heat in the street and the quartet relaxed and spread themselves a little as Skinhead, the bartender, nodded them toward the back room.

Preacher knocked and when a gruff acknowledgement came from within he turned the knob and the four solemnly entered.

High-Queen Teddy was at her usual place at the

round baize-top table with a hand of solitaire spread in front of her. For a few minutes she continued to play her hand, only nodding to them to take chairs.

"Shit." The word came calmly from the lady with the cold cigar clenched in her powerful jaws, and in one swift motion she gathered the cards and folded them into a deck, which she placed in front of her.

There was silence in the room. Teddy looked over at her rocking chair, but didn't move toward it. Her eyes returned to her visitors.

"You want something, Teddy?" Preacher, always the agreeable one, arched his eyebrows as he turned on the unction.

"I want to know why you four clowns are so goddamn dumb. Now you, Preacher, you cut that trying to sweet-Jesus me, understand?"

Preacher, flushing madly, bowed his head in acquiescence. "You sent for us, Teddy," he said, speaking down to his folded hands. "What's wrong?"

"It's draughty in here." High-Queen squirmed in her chair, drawing her wrappings tighter around her body. She took the cigar out of her mouth. "What's wrong! Hell, what isn't wrong! You dumbbells! Can't you deliver to them redskins without the whole fucking world knowing it!"

"But we thought . . ." Sunny Jim started to say.

"You *thought!*" Teddy's eyes rose to heaven, only her gaze met the ceiling, which was also the floor of the room above where Ginger had conducted her vigorous activities with Slocum. Reminded of this, she cursed violently, thinking too of that fool Skinner, who likewise didn't have a brain worth a wooden nickel.

"Teddy." It was Preacher speaking more firmly now,

for he was remembering the place accorded him by Teddy, which was as the go-between with herself and the three wagon men. Preacher liked authority, and sometimes he could live up to it. Aided by his intake of All-Over Cure-all, he now managed to secure a foothold in what was obviously going to be a full-scale assault on the part of High-Queen Teddy and a rushing retreat of the four. "Teddy, I got something to say here. I ain't so sure about selling whiskey to the redskins. Hell, they paint up and hit the path, they'll be chopping everybody to pieces all over this country."

"Bullshit! That's the booze talking, mister. Now shut up and listen to what I am sayin'!"

So ended Preacher Tom's moment. He subsided, to those three words as Teddy now drove in with pick, hammer, and saw.

"You clowns was hired to run a wagon train with whiskey not just for the Injuns, but also for the ranchers, the miners, and the fucking army. Remember! So all right, I did tell you to start packing a few crates of guns to the tribes. But no ammo! I said to each and all of you," She waited, her breath sawing through her irate body as her eyes bulleted each one in turn. "Did I say that, or did I not say that?"

Pause.

"Answer!" The command broke like a rifle shot into the room. And in further emphasis she hit the table top with her palm, like a teacher reprimanding unruly children. As luck would have it, the force of the blow was such that it knocked her cigar off the edge of the table, where she had placed it after removing it from her mouth. This brought forth a string of obscenity which wasn't helped by both Sunny Jim and Saginaw Bill diving to recover the cigar and knocking their heads together.

"Sit down, you fools!" Teddy swiftly regained her calm, and not bothering to even look at the rank stogie, relighted it and settled back in her chair.

"You did say that, Teddy," Preacher said. And he looked at his pals, who all nodded vigorously.

"Then . . . ," The word was almost a whisper, slipping toward the four like a snake. "Then . . . will you tell me how those murdering, thieving, crazy red devils got all that ammo—which *you fools delivered!*" The whisper had grown now to a crescendo of controlled fury as she leaned forward in further emphasis of what she had to say, and then, ending, dropped back into her chair, suddenly calm as a mountain lake. The four were totally unnerved.

Again there was silence in the room.

Teddy smoked her cigar. At one point she looked down at the back of her hand, and after a moment she returned her gaze to the four men, waiting.

At last, Preacher Tom, taking the lead again, said that they had been told by someone to deliver the boxes along with the whiskey and guns. None of them had known what was inside, but the man said that it was orders.

"Who said this?"

"Don't know his name," Saginaw Bill said, and he looked at his companions.

"Never said who he was," Sunny Jim put in.

"What did he look like?"

"Big feller. That feller Slocum braced and pistol-whipped one night. Remember that? You come at him with the shotgun, Teddy. In the poker game."

"You're talking about Carvers."

"Dunno his name."

"You do now. Cole Carvers. That son of a bitch." She wasn't referring to Carvers, but to Mysterious Billy Dime, who clearly had ordered it. "Son of a bitch," she muttered.

"Teddy, we figured it was from you." Charlie O'Moss, met by Teddy's continuing silence, shifted in his chair.

"From now on, you remember that you take orders from me. And only from me."

To their astonishment, the tone was muted, even soft, though no less penetrating. But they were all four experiencing acquittal, and this was enough.

"Now get the hell out of here. But remember...!" And the voice rose, the forefinger drove at them like a gun. "You do not forget that it is me who gives you the orders, not that son of a bitch Carvers, not nobody else either! You got that? You got that!"

Nodding vigorously they rapidly moved to the door of the room and left.

"Jesus God," said Saginaw Bill when they were out in the street. "I could use a drink. But not in there."

Preacher Tom was right with the occasion. "Gentlemen, let us take the wagon down to the livery, and there, in the cool shade of the barn, we can partake of that marvelous life-supporting elixir, All-Over Cure-All. It will prepare us for our later celebration, at which time we can indulge ourselves—if we wish—with good old spirits of grain!"

Laughing with the tremendous relief of their unexpected freedom following their near-brush with total disaster, they climbed into the wagon and headed for the livery.

10

Not everybody knew that T. P. Daventry had a glass eye; and of those who did, most never brought it to mind. T.P. appeared to the citizens of Rock Creek and environs as a solid lawman, capable and honest. And certainly, as far as anyone knew, having but one eye had not hindered his ability with firearms. T.P. himself was seldom unaware of his limitations. But he had learned to take this into account and as a result he had, to his own satisfaction, proven that because he was sightless in one eye he had actually become more capable in his line of work. Still, he did favor his condition by wearing his hat brim low on that side of his face.

One morning T.P. awakened in his rooming house to find something changed in the atmosphere of the town. He knew it was something quite different from the change he had had to get used to after his wife's death, which was also the death of what would have been their first child. Then everything had been different, and it had taken a long while to adjust.

This morning it was different, and yet in a way not completely so. There was the same strange odor of dread and expectancy in the street as he walked down to the eatery for breakfast, that he had known when Ethel had died.

Oliver, the counterman, who rarely spoke, offered the observation that the weather had changed. "Like it's fixin' to storm some. Exceptin' it don't look like it," he added, including the dirty window in his conversation.

T.P. didn't reply and they left it at that. He had some more coffee, built himself a smoke, and when he went out on his rounds he noticed that the saloons appeared more deserted than usual for the early morning. Finished with his rounds, he sat in his office looking at the warrants he had for Mysterious Billy Dime, Cole Carvers, Arkansas Sullivan, Seaborn Quince, and Heavy Hank Perse, each of whom had been recognized at either one of the two train robberies, while Hank had been seen also at the robbery of the Tilghman–Rock Creek stage. The question was where and how to serve them. He still felt his uneasiness of the early morning and when he checked the McCready House and found Slocum gone he felt it more. But which way to go?

The issue was decided for him when around high noon the door of his office opened and a miner named Tom O'Folliard walked in.

"See a whole pack of horsebackers riding pretty hard toward Franc's Peak," Tom said. "Thought you'd better know about that. I ain't mindin' to say who I think they was, but I reckon you can figure."

"The vigilantes."

T.P. looked at the old miner from under the brim of

his Stetson hat, and then offered him a seat. "You look a mite out of breath, Pop. How come? Somethin' else happen?"

"There is action goin' on over to Wagon Box Creek. Wasn't going to bother much about the other bunch, headin' for Franc's Peak; but I run into Sam Olsen— you mind Sam, he hit it real good over at the Tensleep strike. Well, he said he'd heard talk of a strike by Wagon Box Creek. Said the surveyor was out there and found some of the yellow. Looked like it might be a strike." Old Tom raised his longhorn eyebrows, blew between his lips, and, leaning back, slipped his gnarled knuckles under his faded yellow galluses and locked his fingers together on his flat belly.

"That's on Arapaho land," T.P. said.

"So what?"

"So it's Indian territory."

"So was the Black Hills, my friend."

"What are you thinking?" the sheriff asked.

"I am thinking it ain't no time for yours truly to be lollygaggin' around such a vicinity. Hell, I been prospectin' for a new strike over by Franc's Peak, but I'll swear there ain't a thing there. But what I am saying is, between them vigilantes—and there were nigh twenty of 'em, and they were loaded—and them Araps getting feisty; well, it ain't my business, Sheriff."

"It is now," said Daventry, standing up suddenly. "What kind of a horse you got?"

"Crowbait."

"I am deputizing you. You go down to the livery fast. Get the best horse you see there, long as it ain't somebody's, and then hit for McScott; tell Captain Fitzgerald what you told me. He knows the situation here somewhat. Get going."

"Jesus, Sheriff. I ain't . . ."

"You want to wear tin, or just go regular?"

"Shit, I ain't cut out for a lawman, Daventry."

"Do you reckon you're cut out for a corpse? When those boys take over it won't matter. You owe me, god damn it, O'Folliard. You remember that time . . ."

"I got'cha, I got'cha." The miner was already on his feet, remembering all too well the time T.P. had saved his bacon with some of Mysterious Billy's boys.

When he was gone, T.P. checked his weapons, took a sawed-off Greener shotgun out of the gun cabinet, and several rounds of extra ammo for his Winchester and Colt.

As he mounted the blue roan he hoped Fitzgerald would come through. He'd written him, telling him of the growing trouble at Rock Creek, and had kept him informed as other events had developed—the train and stage robberies. He also hoped the army would be there and not out on patrol somewhere. He hoped . . .

To hell with hope, he told himself as he cantered down Main Street, breaking his own rule about running a horse in town and raising all that dust.

Slocum had told both Patches to get on down to the ranch at Jack Creek as soon as they could, but taking care not to be seen. He had reasoned that it would be there that the vigilantes would strike. As he had told Daventry, with the ranch deserted, Dime and his gang would take the position that it was open territory. They must be wondering why they hadn't thought of that before, he told himself as he pushed the buckskin along the hard trail. It was such an obvious way of finding Patches; simply by attracting him.

Yet, there was Henry Skinner. Maybe Skinner had a

wider plan, and had surely thought of getting the ranch simply by occupying "abandoned territory." Probably he was waiting for certain moves to develop in relation to the Indian removal. It wouldn't do to have an outbreak, for instance, and then too he would need the backing of Washington. Yes, that was undoubtedly why he had waited this long. But now, now he had decided on direct action; and perhaps backing had come.

As he rode, Slocum tried to fashion a plan that had been forming in his mind. It was a gamble, but it was the only way they had open. He was counting on nobody knowing there was another way to the JP, over the rimrocks. If he figured correctly, Dime and his gang would come across the Wind Water River and up the narrow trail, which was in full view of the ranch.

It was noon when Slocum reached the spring just below the ranch and dismounted. As far as he could tell, no one was about. That didn't mean, of course, that Jeremy and Dora weren't there. They would be keeping very quiet, out of view of anyone who might come by. On the other hand, they could have been delayed on their way down from the hunting cabin. It was a rough trail, and for much of the way it was necessary to dismount and lead your horse. That would have been tough on Jeremy and would have delayed them.

He listened. Nothing. Only the stirring of the wind. Slocum picketed the buckskin under cover of some pine and fir trees and then walked slowly toward the ranch.

At the edge of the clearing he stopped and took a while to look carefully at everything. He had the definite feeling that somebody was there, and that it was not Jeremy or Dora. Only where? Whoever had set fire to the place had left no building standing. He waited just inside the rim of trees. He waited a long time.

All at once he remembered the root cellar and Grace Patches putting up game and other foods for the time when the weather didn't permit hunting. He could see the place where the root cellar had been, right in back of the cabin. The cabin was a pile of charred logs now, some of which had fallen against the opening to the room that had been dug into the cutbank for food storage. He had noticed the logs before but had not thought particularly of the root cellar.

He remained where he was, hidden from view, watching what he could see of the destroyed ranch. Nothing moved other than wildlife and the wind. Had he been mistaken? He knew himself well enough to know he hadn't. But then where was the danger?

He had just shifted his stance to relax himself a little, for he was beginning to stiffen, when he heard the horse coming up the trail.

Slocum melted even deeper into the foliage, but with a clear view of where he knew the rider had to come. In another minute the man and horse appeared. It was someone he didn't know.

The man rode his little black gelding with the three white stockings right into the clearing where the cabin had stood. Slocum didn't move.

Suddenly a voice called out, "Red! Up here."

And looking up toward the timberline Slocum saw the man approaching with a rifle in his hands. He was afoot.

"What took you so long?"

The man named Red dismounted, and said something that Slocum couldn't hear because the horse was between him and the two men. But now the men came into his direct view as Red's horse moved.

"Anybody here with you?"

"Just little old me. Sure could stand a drink."

The man named Red chuckled. "Finn, boy, I've got just what we need right here. Jesus, how come that Patches built his outfit up here in this godforsaken place!"

"Well, maybe he figgered it was a good place to get hisself buried," the man name Finn replied with a sardonic laugh. "When are the boys coming?"

"They're on their way. What about Patches?"

"The Indian told Dime him and his daughter was on their way down here from wherever they was hid."

"Up by Franc's Peak, I heard."

They had uncorked the bottle and were having a drink, still standing by Red's little black horse.

Finn said, "I bin waiting for them. We better take cover 'fore they get here. They could come any time, I reckon."

"Jesus, whyn't you say that before!" Red, suddenly roused, grabbed the bottle and corked it. "For Christ sake, we mess up on Billy, you know what'll happen!"

"I know what happened when Brady fucked up," Finn said sourly. "Let's get your horse under cover."

Slocum was figuring on the best way to take them, but he hesitated. There was something he didn't like. Something—yes, in Finn's manner. And he remembered something an old Indian had told him long ago. Yellow Hawk, a man he had known in the old days, had taught him a lot of things. The old man had asked him what he would do in a given situation. "Never mind so much what you think the other man will do; but what would *you* do if you were in his feet?"

It had been good advice, like all Yellow Hawk's "advices," as the old man called them. And it had stood Slocum in good stead more than a few times. He remembered it now. What would he do if he was in Finn's shoes, guarding the place until Mysterious Billy Dime's arrival? And he remembered that advice none too soon. For he knew very well what he would do in Finn's shoes.

When he saw the jay take flight from a tree on the other side of where the two men were standing, just beyond the old root cellar, he knew he'd been right. His trail sense had not failed him. The man who stepped out of the trees then was carrying a brand new Spencer repeater.

"Hell, I thought you was alone," Red said to Finn. "Didn't know Macklin was with you."

"Just playin' it careful, Red. Billy told me that trick. Wait a while. See? Anybody following will think it's safe."

Slocum waited another minute until the three had their backs turned to him and were leading Red's horse to the cover of the trees running behind and above the root cellar.

"Is it safe now, boys?" he said, stepping out into full view. "Do not turn around. You're bunched together, and your backs make like almost a single target."

"There is outriders, mister," Finn said.

"No there isn't. Now unbuckle and drop your gunbelts and step away. But still sticking close together."

"Slocum? Are you Slocum?"

"How'd you guess?"

"Listen, Slocum—"

"I said drop your guns, and right now!"

"Slocum, you don't have a chance. Billy and—"

"I know I don't have a chance, mister. But you have got even less of a chance. Now move!"

He marched them to the root cellar, had them tie each

other with the lariat rope taken from Red's horse. He gagged them. He had just finished the job and stepped outside when he heard the horses.

This time it was two and to his relief it was Jeremy and Dora. Quickly he told them what had happened. Jeremy had withstood the trip down from the cabin, and was in good shape. But Dora told him how they had argued about her going to town.

Slocum could hardly take his eyes from the girl. He could feel the attraction between the two of them like hands, like a live thing. And he was thinking how strange it was that in the middle of what was going to be a fight to the death he felt happy. As he led the buckskin and the two Patches horses up to the timberline he saw her looking at him. Her smile was radiant.

"When are they coming?" Slocum had removed the gag from the man named Red but he hadn't untied him. He had loosened his leg ropes so that he could walk outside the root cellar and his companions wouldn't hear the conversation.

"I dunno," Red said.

"Let me," Jeremy said. "I'll make him talk."

Red spat at him and almost before the spittle had landed on its target, Jeremy had slammed him in the pit of the stomach. The big man bent, gagging, and started to throw up.

"Talk!"

"They're on their way. They—they left yesterday. They were gonna stop by at Dutch's place on the way."

"How many?"

"About forty."

"How many?" Slocum said.

"Maybe twenty-five."

"Mysterious Billy with them?" Jeremy wanted to know.

Red nodded.

"Any Shoshone? Any Indian scouting with them?" Slocum asked. Red shook his head. "No."

They tried the other two, both of whom answered without any argument, and the answers were the same.

Meanwhile, Dora had gotten together something to eat.

"They won't come in the night." Slocum said. "And I doubt they'll send any scouts ahead. They're pretty confident, from the looks of things. And that's going to help us."

"I'm glad something's going to help us," Jeremy said sourly.

They ate quickly, and just enough to keep going.

"You get all the sleep you can," Slocum said to Jeremy. To Dora, he said, "I want you to go to town. I can see Jeremy wants that too."

"He spoke of nothing else all the way down here," the girl said. "And I told him no."

"He told me that. But now *I'm* telling you I want you to head into Rock Creek. This is going to be no place for you."

"Sorry. My father is here, and I am staying with him." She glared furiously at both of them. "I thought this had been settled on the way down here." And angrily she stomped away.

Slocum knew he couldn't convince her. After all, the girl was right.

In a minute he called her back. "We've got to work out a plan," he said, taking a completely new tack. "First thing, we've got to find a place up in those rimrocks and get all the dynamite and guns and ammo out of that outhouse and pack it up there."

"What are you figuring, John?" Patches asked.

"I'll explain as we work. We've got to work fast."

In silence they worked hauling the supplies from the outhouse up to the ledge and slit in the rimrocks that Slocum indicated. Then, in the light of the moon, he showed them their positions.

"You take those places. I'll draw them on, and you shoot when they're close enough so you don't miss." He picked up a stick of dynamite. "You had all this damn well wrapped; I hope it's still dry.

"Can't do much else but pray," Jeremy said.

"A sharp eye will help the prayers, I'm sure," Slocum told him. "Look, I'm going to try and find them. I want to know how far away they are and when we can expect them." He stopped suddenly. "By golly, I do believe they could even be coming now, dark or no."

And then the other two heard the horse coming along the hard, thin trail. They were down at the near-empty outhouse now, ready to remove the final load, and they could see the clearing where the cabin and corral had stood. A horse and rider came into view, entering from the direction of the spring.

Slocum leaned toward Jeremy. "Sight on him, but don't shoot. I'm heading down to see how many are with him."

In the next moment he was gone, vanishing into the brush and moving quickly down toward the spring box which the rider had to have passed on his way up. If he was an advance scout, then it would be foolish just to pick him off and give away their surprise.

Slocum had only just gotten on a line with the rider,

who had stopped his horse and was looking around, when he realized who it was.

"You still not taking on any deputies, Sheriff?"

He thought he heard a chuckle start in Daventry's throat, but it died and the man was his old sardonic self.

"Hear you're expecting company up here, Slocum. Whyn't you invite me to the party?"

"Didn't know you liked parties, Sheriff."

"I don't reckon I do like this particular kind, Slocum. But I got some invites in my pocket for some of your guests. They're called warrants."

"My friend, you're going to have about as much chance of serving them as a fart's got in a tornado."

"I am going by the law, Slocum. And this is the way the law does 'er."

"You can help us, Daventry, if you've a mind to. Jeremy and Dora Patches are here with me. And we've got three prisoners in the root cellar. Maybe you'd take a turn at questioning them."

"Good idea. When're you expecting your company?"

"Likely dawn, if they're that close. You see anybody on your way up?"

"Nothing. I only got news from an old miner that he saw Dime and his gang on the move in this direction. That's why I come out here, following from our conversation—you and me—about somebody taking possession here."

"Like I said, Jeremy and Dora are up yonder. Call out when you get up there so they know who you are."

"And you?"

"Checking down below to see where the hell our visitors are coming from—and when."

* * *

It was almost that moment when the sky heralded the very first hint of dawn when Slocum got back up to the rimrocks where he had left Dora and Jeremy. The first person he spotted was Daventry, who was on his turn at sentry. Jeremy, who had taken the first shift, was snoring in his horse blanket, and he found Dora wide awake, lying fully clothed on top of her bedding.

"My heavens, that man Patches snores louder than a buffalo," she said.

They both gave a silent laugh at that.

"I had to move my bed away twice."

"You'd better get some sleep now," Slocum said. "They're just down by the river. They'll be heading up at the first crack of light."

"Do they know we're here?"

"I don't believe so. They might send an advance party up to look around, but then they might just bust on up here. They're pretty confident; and they've been doing a good bit of drinking and a lot of bragging. I guess they figure we're an easy mark."

"How many are there, John?"

"Just the right amount for us to handle."

She had moved a little on her bedroll so that he could sit down beside her. As he did so his hand accidentally brushed her thigh and he felt the tingling go through him.

The next moment he had put his arm around her and held her. With his face in her hair, he felt her fear and her courage both running through her body. He leaned away a little then and touched the side of her face with his first two fingers. "You'd better get some sleep. There isn't much time."

"I don't want to sleep," she said. "Except . . ."

"Except what?" he asked.

"May I tell you another time, John? There's no time now."

"Sure," he said. "Any time." He opened his hand now and held the side of her face lightly, and looked into her eyes. It was still too dark to see clearly, but that wasn't necessary. The feeling was much more clear than any looks.

"I've got to go now," he said. "You and Jeremy take those places I showed you. Get him up the minute it's light if I haven't called you before." He stood up. "I'm going over to talk to Daventry."

"Where will he be placed?" she asked.

"It'll be like this," he said, making an arch of his fingers and thumbs. "They'll come in there, down there at the base. We'll let them come on up to about halfway, where those big clumps of sage are that I showed you. You and Daventry will be there. You'll let them go past you, so that you're covering their rear. Then they'll be up to where we are, myself and Jeremy. Don't fire until I yell."

"But what's going to get them to come up here?" she asked. "All they might want to do is occupy the place where the house and barn were."

"That's what we've got that dynamite for. Daventry and yours truly will be tossing those little bouquets at them. They'll either come up here to get us or they'll have to cut out. Your father is a thoughtful man, Dora. I always said so. Always said he'd make a great sheep-herder, but never had the nerve to tell him to his face." He grinned. "But look, it's a plan he and I worked out when I was here breaking horses with him. And he's been putting dynamite in that outhouse ever since.

There's enough there to blow the top off this mountain."

He wanted to kiss her then, but he didn't; and he wanted to touch her, so he reached out and touched her with his thumb, just on the point of her chin. "I'll be talking to Daventry now," he said. "Think you'd better get your dad up now directly." And he started down to see Daventry.

"What about the prisoners?" Daventry asked when Slocum had finished telling him the plan.

"Did you check them?"

"I did. They offered nothing we didn't know already."

"Then we'll just leave them. You can arrest them," he added quickly.

"That is what I am aimin' to do with the whole outfit," the sheriff said grimly. "And, Slocum, don't you forget for a minute that I am the law."

"I am sure you won't ever let me forget that detail, Sheriff Daventry," Slocum said pleasantly. "And maybe you won't forget that the Patches are fighting for their lives. And their land."

"And you?"

"I am their friend."

"Still not my deputy, eh?"

"I guess you could say I'm my own deputy, Sheriff."

The sun hadn't yet reached over the rimrocks, though its light was filling the sky with the new day when Slocum, stationed down by the spring box, heard the first men and horses. Quickly he got back to Jeremy and Daventry to tell them, and then moved up to the higher rocks, where he saw Dora.

"Just hold your fire, and let them get well inside," he told each of them. "I'll give the signal. Even if you hear the dynamite go off, don't fire until I say."

Daventry started to protest, but Slocum had hurried to his lookout position.

The first riders were already in the clearing where the barn and corral had been and were moving toward the remains of the house.

Slocum was waiting until they were closer together, and right now some of them were drawing in toward Mysterious Billy and the man whom he'd gunwhipped in the Palace de Joy, Cole Carvers. Slocum recognized a few of the others. He was just getting a dynamite stick out of the box he had with him, ready to light it and throw, when he suddenly heard T. P. Daventry's loud voice.

"Dime, you're under arrest, you and your men. Throw down your guns. This is Sheriff Daventry speaking!"

A fusillade of bullets greeted this, and Slocum saw Daventry duck behind a big rock. Slocum didn't even have time to react to the sheriff's unexpected act but lighted and hurled the first stick of dynamite, followed by two, three, and four more. And Jeremy was following suit. The vigilantes were in a turmoil of blasting dynamite, firing wildly at the unseen enemy in the rocks, their horses out of control, with Mysterious Billy roaring orders no one could hear.

"Let them have it!" Slocum roared, and running down to where Daventry had been positioned he grabbed the sticks he had given him and began lighting and throwing them, and T.P. immediately followed suit, almost as though he'd been waiting for permission while Jeremy and Dora both opened fire with their Spencers.

Several of Mysterious Billy's men were down, dead or wounded. Horses were rearing and bucking, and some had been injured by the dynamite, or bullets.

Slocum grabbed his Sharps now and began blasting at whatever target he could find.

It seemed a long time, but he knew later that it had only been moments before the men started dropping their guns.

"There goes Dime!" Jeremy suddenly shouted and he fired after the fleeing horseman. Three others also cut out, their horses flying back down the trail to the river. Slocum could see them clearly as they broke out of the trees below—Arkansas Sullivan, Seaborn Quince, and Cole Carvers, with Mysterious Billy Dime far in front. There was no following them, not with all those prisoners on their hands. Dime and his lieutenants would have to wait.

There were twelve men in the roundup, with three more added from the root cellar. This number didn't include the five dead, but it did count the wounded.

"I can't believe it," Jeremy Patches was saying. "Slocum, you son of a gun, I can't believe it!" His elation had brought him to the edge of tears and hilarity as he stood there with his arm around Dora while Slocum and T. P. Daventry, who was wounded slightly in the arm and nicked along the side of his head, collected the vigilante weapons.

"Well, Slocum, I am still the law. And these men will be jailed until they stand trial."

"I'm all for that, Sheriff. But you should've told me you were going to make an invitation before the fight started. We came close to losing you, damn it."

But Slocum wasn't angry. Even so, Daventry's face reddened and a sheepish grin spread from ear to ear. "I hadn't intended to do that, Slocum. I was planning to go right along with your plan, wholly. But, damn it, I'm a lawman, and you know what that means sometimes. You've been with the law yourself, I know. And there's always the question that if you take the badge you've got to uphold what it stands for."

"I respect that," Slocum said. He held up a stick of dynamite. "But I know it was this that won for us."

"It was John Slocum won it for us," said Jeremy Patches firmly.

The sheriff of Rock Creek nodded in agreement, and turned his good eye toward Slocum. He looked as though he was going to say something.

"Daventry," Slocum said quickly, cutting him off, for he was not one to care for compliments directed toward himself, "I do believe Rock Creek is damn lucky with its choice of sheriff. And that's my last word."

"Maybe," T.P. said, coming in smoothly and grinning. "Maybe. But could be it's me ought to be *your* deputy, Slocum. Turn it over, mister. And that's *my* last word." And with a brisk nod, and a squint from his good eye, he turned to his prisoners.

11

It wasn't finished. Daventry had jailed four of the men whom he considered to be the most dangerous. He had warned the rest that they could get out of the country or face trial when the circuit judge came. As he'd pointed out to a number of citizens, these were the hangers-on; the four in the small jailhouse were the important ones in the vigilantes second echelon; though it was Mysterious Billy, Cole Carvers, Quince, and Arkansas Sullivan who were the main targets.

"All we got to do is get Dime," he told Slocum.

"He'll show up," Slocum said.

"You sound pretty sure."

"Whoever's behind Dime isn't going to give up, and neither is Dime."

His prediction began to prove itself that same evening when the sheriff was drygulched while making his rounds. A rifle shot from a dark alley did it, but luckily the bullet wasn't fatal. It was enough to put the sheriff into bed, and keep him there, however.

"You got to take it now, Slocum," T.P. said, his words coming weakly as he lay in bandages and pain the next morning.

"I reckon you're right, T.P."

"Dime and his boys'll be coming after. You were right."

"You need anything?" Slocum asked.

The wounded man managed a weak grin. "Not with that cute little nurse taking care of me."

Dora, coming into the room, laughed at that. "We'll just see about that," she said. And Slocum could see that her eyes were on him, and his body quickened.

When they were both outside the room he said, "There's still work to do."

"I know. Please, please be careful."

"How's Jeremy?"

"He's fine. I am making him rest. He overdid it out there."

"Keep him and yourself away from the street for the next day or so," Slocum said tersely as he left.

As he started down the street toward the center of town, a voice called him. Turning, he saw it was Ginger. It was early and the street was nearly deserted. He wondered what she could be doing out at that hour, but then thought she might have been waiting for him, for she had come around the corner of the house, as though keeping out of sight.

"Watch out for Skinner," she said, and walked quickly away without looking at him. Yet he had caught the fear in her voice. He watched her turn down another side street.

When he walked into Daventry's office he saw the grey cat sitting on the desk meowing.

"Guess I inherited you too," he said, and began looking for some milk. There wasn't any.

"I'll get you some from the beanery," he said. "So stop complaining."

But first he stepped to the gun cabinet and pulled out the shotgun which he'd taken to the JP fight and hadn't used. He checked the load and placed it on top of the desk. Then he checked his Colt, deciding he'd not take the shotgun on his rounds, figuring it might give some people the frights. But he changed his mind instantly on that. There were, after all, four of those boys, and he had no deputies.

He had just hefted his handgun, checking his draw, when the door opened and in walked Jeremy Patches.

"What are you doing up?" Slocum demanded. "Your daughter said she told you to rest, stay in bed."

"That's right she did. Now shut up a minute and stop being so pigheaded."

Catching it, Slocum said, "What you got?"

"Dime's in town and he's having a big fight with Carvers over at Teddy's about who's going to kill you. They each want the privilege. I mean they are really going at it."

"They drinking?"

"Heavy, from what I hear."

"People know I'm acting as sheriff?"

"They know Daventry's out of it, and there's talk you might be stepping in. Yeah."

"And what about Quince and Sullivan?"

"Haven't seem 'em."

Slocum had his hand on the doorknob. He was looking down at the cat, who had come to rub against his leg. "Cat, you're gonna have to wait a spell for your milk."

"John, there's something smells about it."

"Those two about to have it out?"

"They're talking lead, or were when I left to look for you."

Slocum went quickly again to the gun cabinet. "Take the Winchester," he said. "And keep your eye on the rooflines and alleys; especially the rooflines."

And then they were in the street. He could see Mysterious and Carvers, followed by a small group of excited men, just outside the Palace de Joy. Someone, he couldn't tell who it was, was trying to bring order to the excitement.

"You get across the street," Slocum said and he began walking slowly along the boardwalk.

When he was close enough to the group, none of whom appeared to notice him, he called out, "There'll be no gunfighting this morning, gents."

But the main participants ignored this remark. Cole Carvers's voice cut like a rusty knife into the morning air as he almost screamed, "God damn you, Dime, you son of a bitch, I am going to put air in you right now!"

"And I am puttin' lead in you, you fucker!" Mysterious Billy roared back.

And in another moment they had separated, marked off their prearranged paces, and turned.

"You count, Morgan!" Mysterious Billy snapped.

"Hold it," Slocum said. "And drop your guns!"

Both men turned to face him. And he realized how far apart they were. It had been clever. And with the crowd he couldn't use the shotgun. He knew what was going to happen next, and it did. But a long moment seemed to hold that tableau first. And then Cole Carvers made a mistake and shifted his eyes upward.

Slocum dropped to the ground as the rifleman on the roof fired, missing him by inches. At the same instant both Dime and Carvers drew and fired at him directly; and he heard the Winchester across the street. All of which was lost in the ultimate twin blasts of Slocum's .44. Even before Mysterious Billy Dime and Cole Carvers hit the street, Slocum had rolled and come up behind a verandah post, his eyes sweeping the roofline. He was just in time to see a man pitching down, almost opposite the man in the alley whom Jeremy Patches now took for his second target.

Slocum walked over to the dead Carvers and the dying Mysterious Billy Dime.

"You son of a bitch, Slocum," Billy said. "You've got to be Irish, God damn you." There was a hard grin on his face. That grin froze right there as his last breath left him.

Turning, Slocum saw Jeremy coming toward him. He had accounted for Seaborn Quince and Arkansas Sullivan. He stood looking down at Mysterious Billy Dime.

"Thank God it's over," Jeremy said.

Slocum was about to tell him it wasn't when he heard the woman's scream and his eye caught the movement in the second-floor window of Teddy's place.

Henry Skinner's bullet missed John Slocum by a good couple of feet. It went nowhere. High-Queen Teddy's bullet did not.

Later, High-Queen put it to Slocum in her customary prose. "I didn't do it for you, sweetheart. It's like I don't let no smart-ass son of a bitch treat my girls rough. You get me? I'd of let that old bastard give one black eye to Ginger, but not two!"

"Thank you, John," Dora said as Slocum sat up on the edge of his bed, still looking down at her damp, naked beauty.

"I thank you."

They both had a little laugh at that.

When he lay down again she said, "I thought you were going to get up and get dressed."

"No. Sorry to disappoint you. I only sat up to get a fresh look at you."

"Well, maybe I'd like a fresh look at you," she said. And she was up on her hands and knees. "And at him." Her hand was already holding his rigid organ. And now she bent down, taking it deep into her mouth and throat.

Slocum thought he would explode any second, but she seemed to know how to ease away just at the moment when he would have come. Finally he rolled her over and mounted her, going all the way. Stroking gently, then more quickly, but always with gentleness, he rode her all the way to the moment when their bodies took over, and neither had anything to say about the ultimate coming.

JAKE LOGAN